'The papers called you—they called you the "Thief of Hearts". They said you—you stole jewels from women you . . . you'd . . .'

Saxon laughed. 'Hearsay, Miss Mitchell.' A quick, sexy smile curved across his mouth. 'Believe me,' he said softly, 'I've never taken anything from a woman that she didn't offer gladly.'

The taunt brought a rush of colour to Sara's cheeks, and he smiled wolfishly. 'Are you afraid I'll steal something else, then?' His eyes moved slowly, insolently, over her, lingering on her unpainted lips, moving to her breasts, which were falling and rising rapidly beneath the bulky sweater. 'Hell, it might be interesting, Sara.' His gaze rose to meet hers; she saw a sudden blaze of light deep within the brown depths. 'Very interesting,' he said softly.

FLY LIKE AN EAGLE

BY

SANDRA MARTON

MILLS & BOON LIMITED
ETON HOUSE   18-24 PARADISE ROAD
RICHMOND   SURREY   TW9 1SR

*First published in Great Britain 1989
by Mills & Boon Limited*

© Sandra Myles 1989

*Australian copyright 1989
Philippine copyright 1989
This edition 1989*

ISBN 0 263 76498 2

*Set in Times 10 on 11 pt.
01 – 8912 – 57711*

Typeset in Great Britain by JCL Graphics, Bristol

Made and Printed in Great Britain

CHAPTER ONE

SARA MITCHELL looked up from her desk as the outer door to the Brookville police station opened. The pages of the calendar on the wall behind her lifted as the frigid breath of January blew into the already chilly room. Sara shivered dramatically, and dipped her head in greeting to the heavy-set man standing in the doorway.

'Good morning, Chief. Welcome to Siberia.'

The man grunted as he shouldered the door shut. 'Don't tell me,' he said grumpily. 'The heat's gone off again, right?'

Sara sighed as she pushed her chair back and rose from her desk. 'No, it's working. I guess the furnace just can't keep up with the cold.' Her dark blue eyes lit with amusement as the man began struggling out of his sheepskin jacket.

'You look just like a bear in that thing, Chief.'

Jim Garrett grinned as he hung the jacket on a rack beside the door. 'And it's not police issue. Yeah, I know. But it keeps me warm.' He shuddered and rubbed his hands together. 'What's the weather forecast for tonight? Do you know?'

Sara nodded. 'Yes,' she said, reaching for the Pyrex coffee-pot near her desk. 'I caught it on the radio about an hour ago. Believe me, you don't want to hear it.'

Her boss groaned softly. 'More snow?' he muttered.

She nodded again. 'More snow. And freezing temperatures. And sleet. And——'

Jim Garrett shook his head. 'Spare me the details, Sara.' He smiled gratefully as he reached for the steaming mug of coffee she held out to him. 'Thanks,' he said, wrapping his meaty hands around it. 'The thought of your coffee's the only thing that got me here this morning.'

Sara smiled. 'I'll bet. I don't suppose Alice's pancakes had a part in it, hmm?'

Her boss grinned. 'Well, sure they did. But my wife's only responsible for getting me out the door. My secretary's responsible for getting me through the day.' Jim's good-natured smile vanished. 'Damn,' he said, staring out of the window at the snow falling steadily from a leaden sky. 'I just wish to hell the Winstead party wasn't tonight.'

Sara's eyebrows rose. 'Or any other night.'

Jim Garrett blew on the hot coffee, then took a cautious sip. 'Yeah, but you can't much blame me, can you? Baby-sitting three million bucks' worth of jewels isn't my idea of police work.'

'Five million,' Sara said with a teasing smile. 'According to today's paper, the Maharanee of Gadjapur's jewels are worth five million dollars. The diamond tiara alone——'

'Please!' Jim held up his hand. 'Spare me the details, huh? I am positively, absolutely overdosed on those damned jewels. I've been listening to Simon Winstead prattle on about them for weeks. Diamond tiaras, emerald necklaces, rubies and pearls and sapphires . . .' He made a face and held out his empty mug. 'Don't look at me like that, Sara. I know one cup's all I'm supposed to have, but on a day like this, what does it matter? I'm going to have an ulcer the size of New York City by the time this damned party's over.'

'It's all in a good cause,' she said mildly. 'The paper says——'

'I know what it says. It says Winstead Jewellers

bought the Maharanee of Gadjapur's jewels; it says they're loaning them to the Fine Arts Museum for exhibit; it says that tonight the *crème de la crème* of New York society is gonna pay a hundred bucks a head to crowd into Simon Winstead's fancy house up on Stone Mountain, so they can stand on each other's toes and gawk at the jewels close up, before the museum gets 'em tomorrow.' Jim swallowed a mouthful of coffee. 'It's what the paper doesn't say that worries me.'

Sara sighed and sat down at her desk. 'The house is like a fortress. You said so yourself. An electronic gate. An electronically controlled safe. Private guards. The state police have been notified. And you'll be there——'

'Yeah. Me and Brookville's five other cops.' The chief grimaced. 'Well, at least the weather's on our side. A thief would have to be out of his mind to try anything when the roads are clogged with snow. Which reminds me, Sara, you'd better call Hank and tell him to sand the Stone Mountain road just before this thing's due to start. Half the people coming to this shindig are from the city; New Yorkers don't have the damnedest idea how to drive on ice or snow. Call Tommy, too. Tell him to get his plough out here and——'

Sara smiled. 'I already have.'

'And give Jack Barnes a ring. See if you can talk him into keeping the garage open late. Tell him——'

'I called him a few minutes ago. He says he'll have the tow-truck on stand-by.'

Jim Garrett raised his grizzled eyebrows. 'You're as good at this job as I am, Sara Mitchell.' He smiled as he put down his empty mug. 'And you make a mean pot of coffee. What am I going to do if the good people of Brookville find out it's really you who's running this department?'

Sara laughed softly. 'We just won't tell them,' she

said. 'Let them go on thinking I'm only your secretary. Which reminds me—I typed up the final guest-list you wanted. It's on your desk.'

The chief nodded. 'Fine. I'll take a look at it first thing.' He started towards his office, then paused and looked at Sara speculatively. 'You sure you don't want to come to this damn fool party tonight, Sara? Alice and I would be happy to take you with us.'

Sara had a sudden vision of herself in a brightly lit ballroom, surrounded by elegantly gowned women and handsomely dressed men. The thought was as frightening as it was exciting, and she shook her head.

'No, thank you, Jim.' She gave him a quick smile. 'You can tell me all about it tomorrow.'

Her boss sighed as he opened the door to his office. 'Right. Well, maybe the bad weather will keep the crowd down.' He looked at Sara's raised eyebrows. 'You don't think so, hmm?'

She shook her head again. 'I wish I could say I did, Chief. But there's been too much publicity about this party—it has turned into the charity event of the season.'

Jim nodded. 'The advertising gimmick of the season, you mean. Our little department's gonna work itself silly providing security so that Simon Winstead can get himself and his store a load of free publicity.'

'The ticket proceeds are going to the children's home.'

'Yes, yes, that's what Winstead keeps telling me. But that doesn't mean I have to like him, or his party. If anything should go wrong——'

Sara nodded, although she was barely listening. Her boss had been making the same speech every day for the past month. She couldn't fault him for worrying—Jim Garrett had been chief of police in Brookville for as long as she could remember, and he was dedicated to his job. But his department's law-enforcement duties dealt mostly with family disputes, disorderly behaviour, and the occasional drunk driver. There would probably be more than one or two of those to deal with tonight, after the party, but nothing worse. Jim had inspected the Winstead house the week before, and pronounced its electronic security systems a marvel. Even the insurance company . . .

Sara held up her hand. 'I almost forgot. General Casualty called a while ago. They said to tell you they're sending someone to represent them tonight.'

The chief frowned. 'Terrific. What's the guy going to do? Sell insurance to Winstead's society pals?'

Sara grinned. 'I don't think that's quite the idea, Chief. He's some kind of security expert. They said he was their consultant when the electronic devices were installed.'

Jim ran his hand through his greying hair. 'Just what I need. Some four-eyed whiz-kid underfoot tonight. All right, what's the guy's name?'

'I wrote it down right—here it is. Saxon. Peter Saxon. They said he'll be here some time this afternoon.'

Jim Garrett's forehead creased. 'Saxon, hmm? Hell, that name sounds familiar . . .' He sighed and shook his head. 'Let me know when he gets here, Sara. I don't want to see him until I've finished going through that guest-list one last time.'

Sara nodded solemnly. 'No one gets past me, Chief,' she said, and she flashed him a quick smile. 'I'll guard the door to the *sanctum sanctorum* with my life.'

Her boss grinned as he closed the door to his private office behind him. Silence settled over the main room, broken only by the hiss of the overworked radiator and the occasional wail of the wind outside. Sara sat at her

desk and rolled a sheet of paper into her typewriter.
There were half a dozen letters to get out, mostly
reminders to the local merchants that they had agreed to
a temporary no-parking zone along Main Street. When
she finished those, there were a couple of bulletins to
hang on the wall behind her desk, photos and
descriptions of criminals that had come in the morning's
mail.

Sara always put them up. This was, after all, a police
station, despite the fact that Chief Garrett dissuaded
most people from filing formal complaints until they
had talked their problems out. Brookville lay just north
of New York City and its problems—too far to be
within comfortable commuting distance, except for the
half a dozen wealthy New Yorkers who had built homes
here recently, willingly trading distance for the town's
quiet charm.

Sara sighed as she pulled a completed letter from the
typewriter. Maybe that was why the Winstead party had
attracted so much attention. The famous jeweller's
home stood on a mountain overlooking the town, an
object of conjecture ever since it had risen above the
valley a few months ago. When he had announced that
his world-famous Fifth Avenue shop had bought the
Maharanee of Gadjapur's jewels, and would show them
at his home on this night, an almost palpable excitement
had gripped the town.

People had jockeyed for ways to attend. Except for
the Garretts, no one Sara knew had been invited. But
there were other ways to get through the door—the
caterer had recruited servers and cooks, maids and
cleaners. Everyone wanted to see the Winstead house,
the fabulous jewels, and the 'select few' invited to the
party.

Sara smiled to herself as she rolled another piece of

paper into the typewriter. The 'select few' was, apparently, going to number in the hundreds.

'Everyone who's anyone,' Alice Garrett had said happily the other day when she'd tried to convince Sara to come to the party. 'You'd have such a wonderful time, Sara. Haven't you ever dreamed of going to a ball?'

Sara had. She had dreamed of lots of things—of leaving the town where she'd spent her life, of doing something more exciting than sitting at this old Underwood typewriter day after day, of meeting a man who would see beyond her quiet exterior to the woman trapped within, who was eager for life. But that had been long ago, before she learned that dreams were, after all, flimsy creations of the imagination that collapsed when you tried to live them.

Sara had been a shy child; her mother, an embittered widow, had talked about her father in such bitter tones, it was almost as if Eli Mitchell's death when Sara was just a baby had been a deliberate plot to get back at his young wife and daughter. She had raised Sara with such a fierce protectiveness that it had locked out the rest of the world.

And she'd been right to do so. Sara had learned that the hard way.

'Go on, make a fool of yourself,' Beverly Mitchell had said, when a wistful Sara decided to go to her high-school graduation party.

No one had asked her to go, of course. She'd never had a date in her life, which, her mother insisted, was all for the best. But some girls were going alone, and Sara had taken her courage in hand and decided she would, too.

The party was years behind her, but the pain of standing alone beside the dance-floor, a painful smile pasted to her lips while she waited, without hope, for someone—anyone—to ask her to dance, was still as vivid as if it had happened yesterday.

Sara had only tried to live one dream after that, and the memory of where it had led was still almost more than she could bear. The day after high-school graduation, she'd told her mother that she wanted to look for a job and an apartment in New York City. Beverly Mitchell had been appalled.

'Leave me, Sara? Leave your home? Are you crazy?'

Somehow, Sara had stood up to her mother, as if she knew in her heart that she would either begin to live her own life now, or lose the chance forever. She had risen early each morning and caught the train into Manhattan, trying not to let her mother's tight-lipped silences erode her determination. And then—then there had been the day she'd come home, all excited about a job offer. She had been in the midst of telling a white-faced Beverly Mitchell about it, when her mother had swayed and fallen to the floor.

The doctors had insisted that the terrible, wasting illness that had struck was something that her mother had been incubating for a long time.

'It has nothing to do with you, Sara,' old Dr Harris had said impatiently.

Sara told herself he was right. But it didn't matter. By the time she had nursed her mother through the horrible years preceding her death, all her dreams had faded, until now they were like the corsage she'd bought herself the day of that long-ago high-school party—pale and brittle, and only a faint reminder of what might have been.

Until the last few days. For some unknown reason, she had begun to feel a strange restlessness. She found herself awakening during the night, unable to recall the dreams that had made her twist in her narrow bed, knowing only that they left her with a strange feeling of discomfort, of something half-finished or, perhaps, not yet begun . . .

The outer door banged open and a sudden blast of frigid air swept into the room. Sara looked up in surprise.

A man stood in the open doorway, silhouetted against the leaden sky. He was tall and lithe, impeccably dressed in an expensive grey overcoat worn open over a darker grey suit. Flakes of snow were sprinkled on his dark, thick hair and, as she watched, he raised his hand and ran long, tapered fingers through it. He had dark eyes, a straight nose and a wide moustache.

The kind gunfighters wore in films about the Old West, Sara thought crazily, and her heart made a strange leap within her chest.

You've been working at this job too long, Sara.

She smiled politely. 'Good morning. May I——'

He slammed the door shut, cutting her off in mid-sentence. His glance fell on her, then swept past her with insolent ease. She felt the quick rise of colour to her cheeks. There was no question but that he had dismissed her as readily as if she were a piece of furniture.

'Yes,' he said, moving towards her, 'you may. Tell the chief that I'm here.'

His voice was low-pitched, its tone as arrogant as the expression on his face. Sara drew in her breath.

'Do you have an appointment?' she asked coolly.

A brilliant question, Sara. Of course he hasn't; you make all the appointments here. What in heaven's name is wrong with you? And why—why does this man look so familiar?

A cool smile curved across his lips. 'I don't need one,' he said carelessly. 'Just tell him——'

Sara's eyes narrowed. 'I hate to disappoint you, but you do, indeed, need an appointment. Chief Garrett is very busy. He——'

The man laughed. His teeth, Sara noticed, were very white against his tanned skin.

'Look, sweetheart——'

'My name is Miss Mitchell,' Sara said, even more coldly. 'I'm the chief's secretary.'

His eyes lit with amusement. 'And a formidable one you are, Miss Mitchell,' he said, as his gaze moved slowly over her.

For an instant, Sara saw herself as she knew he must—the pale hair neatly clasped at the nape of her neck, the shapeless wool sweater, the tweed skirt. She felt the heat rushing to her cheeks again, and anger flooded through her.

'What is it you want, Mr . . .?'

The man grinned. 'Do you always guard your boss's door with such determination, Miss Mitchell?'

Sara's blush deepened. *I'll guard your door with my life,* she'd told Jim. Why was it that, when *she* had said the words, they had sounded like a joke, but when this . . . this stranger said something similar, it sounded almost pathetic?

'Are you always so rude?'

The words were out before she could stop herself. The man laughed and shook his head.

'*Touché,* Miss Mitchell. Look, why don't we begin again? I'll go outside, open that door, step into the office, and——'

'And we'll be nowhere unless you tell me your name and——'

'Saxon. Peter Saxon. General Casualty sent me. I'm here to check on the Winstead security arrangements.'

Sara stared at him. Some four-eyed whiz-kid, the

chief had said, but that hardly described Peter Saxon. In fact, it was impossible to picture him working for something so conservative as an insurance company. The gunfighter's image flashed into her mind again, and she shook her head impatiently. Why did she keep thinking that? And where had she seen this man's face before? Where?

'When you've finished committing my features to memory, Miss Mitchell, I'd appreciate it if you would buzz your boss and tell him I'm here.'

Her cheeks turned scarlet, and she pushed back her chair and rose to her feet.

'Just have a seat,' she said stiffly. 'I'll see if the chief——'

Peter Saxon rolled his eyes skyward. 'Hell, it's got to be easier to get into the Oval office!'

'Chief Garrett is busy. I'll tell him——'

Peter Saxon moved towards her. 'I'll tell him myself,' he said impatiently. His hands closed on her arms, and he lifted her out of his way as easily as if she were weightless.

'Mr Saxon! What do you think you're——?'

The door to the chief's office sprang open. Jim Garrett glowered at Sara, then at the man beside her.

'Is there a problem out here, Sara?'

Sara swallowed. 'This man—this man is from the insurance company. His name is——'

'My name is Saxon. General Casualty asked me to drop by and see you before I went out to the Winstead house.'

Garrett's eyes narrowed speculatively, as if he, too, were trying to place Peter Saxon's face, and then he shrugged his shoulders and turned towards his office.

'Well, come on in and we'll talk.'

'Jim,' Sara said quickly, 'I'm sorry. I tried——'

A lazy smile eased across Saxon's mouth. 'That's all right, sweetheart,' he said softly, touching his hand lightly to her cheek, 'I'll tell your boss you fought like a tiger. Don't worry about a thing.'

She watched in stunned silence as the door swung shut. Her hand rose slowly to her face, and she put her fingers against her cheek. The skin seemed to burn where Peter Saxon had touched it.

She was trembling when she sat down at her desk. Half a dozen angry retorts sprang into her mind, and she wished she had thought of them a moment before. But how could she have? Saxon had caught her by surprise. Anyway, she wasn't used to that kind of thing, that teasing she knew went on between men and women. Saxon had to know it; that had to have been why he had done it, just to make her feel uncomfortable . . .

Voices drifted from behind the closed door. Jim's voice was loud and angry, which surprised her. In the seven years she had worked for him, she'd rarely seen him lose his temper. Now, she could hear Peter Saxon's voice, too. The laughter had fled it, and he sounded as angry as Jim.

Sara pushed back her chair, uncertain as to what to do, just as the door to the chief's office was flung open. Her boss stalked towards her, his normally florid face almost purple with rage.

'Get me Dick Parker at General Casualty,' he demanded.

She stared past him to the doorway, where Peter Saxon stood, arms crossed. The lazy, insolent smile was gone. Beneath the moustache, his mouth was narrow with anger. His eyes were dark coals in his face. There was, Sara thought suddenly, a look of closely controlled violence about him. His well-tailored clothing still fitted his lithely muscled body with refined ease, but it seemed out of place. It was as if a leopard had tried to put on a sheepskin.

'Dammit to hell, Sara, get me that number!'

Her hands shook as she dialled, then handed Jim the phone. She heard him snarl into it, but his words didn't penetrate. Her eyes were locked on Peter Saxon's face. Of course she had seen him before. In a newspaper? A magazine? Yes, in both places. But why? Why . . .?

Jim Garrett cursed, snarled something into the phone, then slammed it down. His breathing was rapid and loud.

'Terrific,' he said. 'That's terrific. Just what I needed.'

Saxon shrugged his shoulders. A smile curved across his mouth, but his eyes remained dark and cold.

'The company thinks so.'

Jim Garrett laughed mirthlessly. 'So they just said. And that stupid S.O.B. Winstead thinks so, too, I suppose.'

Saxon nodded. 'He says it will bring in a lot of publicity. More tickets. More money for the charity.'

Jim slammed his hand against Sara's desk. 'And you, friend, probably love every minute of all this. Hell, I'll bet you're eating it up.'

Peter Saxon's smile wavered, and then he shrugged again. 'It's—interesting.'

The police chief laughed unpleasantly. 'Interesting? Giving you this job is like asking a fox to guard a henhouse.'

Saxon's eyes met Garrett's. 'Their reasoning precisely.' The cold, quick smile came and went again. 'What better way to protect the chickens than to ask the fox's opinion of the henhouse?'

Jim's lip curled in disgust. 'Listen, Saxon, you may have conned General Casualty, you may have conned

Winstead, you may have conned your parole officer . . .'

Sara drew in her breath. 'Parole officer?' she whispered.

'. . . but I wasn't born yesterday. And if you think I'm going to turn you loose in that house tonight——'

'It's not your decision, Garrett. Winstead and the company want me there. I'm the man who chose the security systems——'

Jim laughed coldly. 'Right. I almost forgot that. Hell, who'd believe this?'

Sara cleared her throat. 'Chief, please, what's this all about?' Jim Garrett spun towards her. 'I'll be out all afternoon, Sara. I'm going to accompany Mr Saxon while he checks out the Winstead house.'

'You have appointments later, Jim. And——'

'Mr Saxon's my only appointment today, Sara. I'm going to stick to him like glue. And tonight——' The chief's eyes narrowed. 'Damn,' he muttered. 'Tonight's impossible. How am I going to supervise my men and those private cops Winstead hired, and still stay with Saxon?'

Peter Saxon's smile was icy. 'You can spare me the hospitality, Garrett. I don't need an escort.'

Jim stabbed his finger at Sara. 'You're working tonight,' he said curtly.

Sara blinked. 'What?'

'You're going to that damned party, Sara.'

She shook her head. Nothing that was happening made any sense—this least of all.

'I told you, I'm not. Thank you for asking, but——'

Jim Garrett slammed his hand against her desk so hard that she jumped. 'Dammit, Sara, this isn't an invitation, it's an order. Give Saxon your address.'

Her eyes widened with bewilderment. 'What? What are you talking about? I don't——'

Saxon laughed softly. 'What a nice guy you are, Garrett. You're fixing me up with a date. That's decent, I must say.'

'Chief . . .' Sara's voice caught; she cleared her throat and began again. 'Chief, please, what's going on? What are you talking about? I don't understand——'

'Mr Saxon is General Casualty's idea of a security expert, Sara.' Jim's voice was thick with displeasure. 'Would you like to tell her your credentials, Mr Saxon?'

Peter Saxon's brown eyes narrowed. 'No,' he said softly, 'I wouldn't want to spoil things for you, Garrett. Why don't you tell her yourself?'

Jim put his hands on his hips. 'He's a con, Sara. He——'

Sara stared at Peter Saxon in disbelief. He made her a mocking bow.

'An ex-convict, Miss Mitchell. I paid my debt.'

The chief of police snorted. 'He served sixteen months on a four-year term, Sara. Hell, they should have locked him away forever. He's got a list of thefts as long as your arm.'

'I was charged with one count of burglary. The rest is all conjecture.'

Sara let out her breath. 'Yes!' she whispered. 'Your face—I remember now.' She looked at him and swallowed. 'The papers called you—they called you the "Thief of Hearts". They said you—you stole jewels from women you . . . you'd . . .'

Saxon laughed. 'Hearsay, Miss Mitchell.' A quick, sexy smile curved across his mouth. 'Believe me,' he said softly, 'I've never taken anything from a woman that she didn't offer gladly.'

Sara's heart stumbled against her ribs. It had all come tumbling back. The gushing headlines, the swirl of gossip—Peter Saxon, born to wealth and power, had been caught making his way across the dark rooftop of a Sutton Place townhouse with a fortune in emeralds in his pocket. The circumstances of the theft had convinced the police he was the man who had committed a series of breathtaking thefts.

But they could prove nothing. It had even been difficult to get the woman whose emeralds he had just stolen to testify against him. She was a well-known society beauty; she and Saxon had moved in the same circles. She'd claimed that she had been in bed, asleep, when the thief entered her bedroom, that she knew nothing the prosecution could use. The papers had made much of that.

Peter Saxon's voice was a purr. 'You have such an open face, Miss Mitchell. I can tell everything you're thinking.'

Sara blinked, met the laughter in his eyes, and looked at her boss.

'You're crazy, Jim,' she said flatly. 'I'm not——'

'Are you afraid of me, Miss Mitchell?'

Her chin lifted and she turned towards Saxon.

'No,' she said coldly.

Jim Garrett nodded. 'That's my girl. Just don't let him out of your sight, Sara. Wherever he goes, you go.'

Saxon grinned. 'Ah, the possibilities, Miss Mitchell.'

The police chief's face hardened. 'I don't want this creep out of your sight.'

The smile fled from Saxon's lips. 'Don't push me, Garrett,' he said softly. 'I'm here on business. Legitimate business. If you don't like it, take it up with Winstead and the insurance company.'

The portly chief of police stared into Peter Saxon's hard eyes for what seemed forever, and then he swallowed and looked away. A chill raced along Sara's spine, and she knew that what he had seen in those smoky brown irises frightened him as much as it had frightened her.

'Give him your address, Sara. He'll pick you up at seven.'

Sara shook her head. 'Jim, please, you can't ask me to do this. I——'

Garrett waved his hand in dismissal, stepped into his private office, and slammed the door closed. In the sudden silence, Sara and Peter Saxon stared at each other.

'I'm not going with you,' she said.

'You're going.' His voice was flat, and as sharp as the snap of a whip. 'I'm supposed to be in the Winstead house tonight. If you're not with me, stuck to my side like glue, as your boss so graciously put it, I'm going to have a problem gaining entrance.'

Sara's chin lifted. 'I don't give a damn, Mr Saxon. Your problems are not my——'

She gasped as his hands closed on her shoulders. The sudden press of his fingers was like steel.

'Are you afraid I'll steal your jewellery, Miss Mitchell?' His voice was soft, his words a teasing caress.

The taunt brought a rush of colour to her cheeks. 'Don't be ridiculous. I haven't any jewels——'

He smiled wolfishly. 'Are you afraid I'll steal something else, then?' The colour in her cheeks darkened, and he laughed. 'You're the one who brought my nickname into the conversation, sweetheart.' His eyes moved slowly, insolently, over her, lingering on her unpainted lips, moving to her breasts, which were falling and rising rapidly beneath the bulky sweater. 'Hell, it might be interesting, Sara.' His gaze rose to meet hers; she saw a sudden blaze of light deep within the brown depths. 'Very interesting,' he said softly.

The breath caught in her throat. She felt her whole

body begin to tremble, as if she were standing in the wind that blew with increasing strength outside.

'Stop it,' she whispered. 'You have no right . . .'

His hands tightened on her. 'You *are* afraid, aren't you?'

Her heart was hammering so loudly, she was afraid he could hear it, but she shook her head.

'No,' she said quickly. 'Why should I be?'

Peter Saxon smiled crookedly. His eyes darkened until they were like brown velvet, and he drew her to him.

'I don't know,' he said softly. 'Suppose you tell me.'

Sara cried out as his head dipped towards her. 'Don't,' she said, but it was too late. His arms encircled her and drew her to him, as his mouth took hers.

His lips were cool, assured. She could feel his hands spread on her back, feel the heat of his fingers and palms burn through her heavy sweater. Her hands balled into fists as she raised them and forced them against his chest.

'You pig,' she whispered against his mouth. 'You——'

Later, Sara would wonder if everything that happened during the next endless days could be traced to that moment. If she hadn't fought him, if she had simply let him press his unwelcome kiss against her closed mouth, would it all have ended before it began?

She would never know. She would know only that her whispered curse gave him access to her parted lips, that when his mouth took hers again, she felt the sudden, silken brush of his tongue.

She froze for a moment, stunned, and then a heat, so intense that it was beyond anything she had ever known, even in the privacy of her dreams, swept through her.

Her body seemed to become boneless. She trembled

in Peter Saxon's arms; her hands opened and spread on his chest, her fingers curling into the lapels of his coat for support. She heard herself whimper softly, heard him make an answering sound deep in his throat, and then his arms tightened around her, and he gathered her to him so closely that she could feel the muscled hardness of his body pressing against hers.

In that long, sweet moment, time stopped. Then, with a suddenness that left Sara gasping, Peter's arms fell away from her.

She opened her eyes slowly and stared at him. His face was pale beneath its tan; she wondered if he was as staggered by what had happened as she was.

But then that lazy smile spread across his mouth, and she knew that he was laughing at her, that he had been laughing all the time. 'I'll pick you up at seven sharp, sweetheart.' The smile widened until it was a grin. 'Wear something pretty, hmm? Something blue, to go with those midnight eyes of yours.' Before she could pull away, he reached behind her and pulled the clasp from her hair. It tumbled to her shoulders and he smiled. 'That's better,' he said. 'I like my women with their hair down.'

His insolence galvanised her. '*Your* women?' she said, pulling free of him at last. 'Just who in hell do you think you——?'

But her taut, angry little speech was pointless. The door to the street opened, then closed again.

Peter Saxon was gone.

CHAPTER TWO

THE WINSTEAD house stood at the very top of Stone Mountain. Built of native fieldstone and oak, it had been designed so that, at first glance, it seemed a natural part of the mountain-top. The view it commanded of the valley below would be magnificent, Sara knew. As a child, she had often walked the dirt trail that snaked up the mountain's heavily forested slopes.

'It's too dangerous,' her mother would have said, had she known of these little excursions.

But she never knew, and Sara had loved them. Alone, so close to the sky that she felt she might almost touch the clouds, her childish imagination had turned tree-tops into turrets, and she had dreamed of being a princess in a far-away land. For a child as lonely and alone as Sara, the mountain-top had been a welcome refuge.

She hadn't walked the mountain in years—certainly not since the Winstead house had been built and the dirt trail changed into a private macadam road. The curious and the uninvited—'the great unwashed', Alice Garrett called them with a wry smile—were not welcome at the Winstead estate. A lot of speculation had gone into trying to decide what the huge mansion behind the stone walls was like; townsfolk who worked for the jeweller dropped tantalising hints about Swedish crystal chandeliers, glove-leather furniture, even a greenhouse that contained an indoor pool as well as a jungle of exotic orchids.

'Just think, Sara, the next time the Women's Auxiliary

24

meets, you and I will knock 'em dead with little titbits about the house,' Alice had said that afternoon when she had stopped by the office, and then she'd smiled wickedly. 'Is Peter Saxon as good-looking as his photographs?'

Sara had stared at the older woman. 'Doesn't it bother you that the man's a crook, Alice?'

Alice laughed and slipped her arm around Sara's shoulders. 'You've been working for my husband so long that you're beginning to sound like him! The man works for an insurance company, dear. What could be more conservative?' She had given Sara a quick, affectionate hug. 'You'll be perfectly safe—he's a thief, Sara, not a killer. Besides, there'll be lots of people at the party. What could happen to you?'

'Nothing,' Sara had said quickly, trying not to remember the way she had reacted to Peter Saxon's unwanted kiss. 'But——'

'But nothing, Sara. You're going to the party of the year with someone famous. What could be bad about that?'

Now, staring at the dresses hanging in her wardrobe, Sara gave a deep sigh. Alice had made it sound as if she and Peter Saxon were going out on a date, but she always romanticised things. The bald truth was that this was a command performance, brought on as much by her own stubbornness as by Jim Garrett's instructions. She couldn't have refused to go with Peter Saxon—not after the challenge he had thrown down.

'Are you afraid of me?' he'd asked, with that damnable grin on his handsome face, and then he'd kissed her and embarrassed her and . . .

Sara reached into the wardrobe, deliberately pushing aside the one blue dress she owned. She pulled a beige dress from its hanger and looked at it critically. She'd bought it two years ago, to wear to Jim's and Alice's twenty-fifth anniversary party. It wasn't dressy enough for tonight, but that was fine with her. This was an assignment, nothing more.

Peter Saxon had made a fool of her this morning. Well, tonight she would show him the stuff she was really made of. Nothing he did or said would ruffle her. He could tease her all he liked: she would simply do her job, which was to watch him as he watched the jewels.

She looked into the mirror as she smoothed down the skirt of the beige dress. The colour was too pale for her, the lines too severe. But, with her hair loose and curling from the shower, it looked almost attractive.

'I like my women with their hair down.'

Peter Saxon's voice was as clear as if he were standing in the room beside her. Sara drew in her breath, snatched a tortoiseshell barrette from the dresser, and clipped her hair at the nape of her neck.

If she had anything to say about it, he was in for a long, unsatisfying evening. She would, indeed, stick to him like glue, and even if the insurance company and Simon Winstead were right, even if it weren't necessary for her to keep him from theft, she would certainly keep him from something else.

Peter Saxon might have given up stealing gems, but instinct told her he'd not given up stealing hearts. But not tonight, Sara thought with grim satisfaction. Tonight, he would have her beside him. And she would be a visible reminder to everyone in that house perched on top of Stone Mountain that Peter Saxon was nothing but an ex-convict with a taste for danger and women. If that didn't cramp his style, nothing would.

A couple of hours later, Sara wondered how she could have been so naïve. No, she thought, standing beside

Peter Saxon like a moth beside a butterfly, not naïve.
Stupid was a much better word to use. The Winstead
party was in full swing, the brightly lit rooms crowded
with the rich and the famous, and she'd learned, over
and over again, that all of them, men and women alike,
wanted to meet Peter Saxon and shake his hand.

No, that wasn't quite accurate. The men wanted that.
But the women—the women wanted something very
different. The ones who already knew him—and there
were many of those—threw their arms around his neck,
squealed his name with delight and touched their glossy
mouths to his. The ones who'd never met him before
smiled into his brown eyes, and wordlessly offered him
everything a man could possibly desire. Tall, handsome,
dressed in a black dinner-suit and ruffled shirt that only
emphasised his masculinity, he was, as Jim had said, a
celebrity who stood out even in this famous crowd.

Sara's presence was no detraction at all. She might as
well be invisible, she thought, as yet another Buffy or
Muffy with artfully windblown hair and the scent of
two-hundred-dollar-an-ounce perfume drifting after her
called out Peter's name and launched herself into his
arms. The girl glanced at Sara and then away, the look
telling her more clearly than words that she wasn't
worth worrying about. The man with her looked at Sara
almost kindly, and she stiffened.

Don't feel sorry for me, she thought angrily. This
wasn't like that long-ago, terrible night of her high-
school dance. She was as out of place now as she had
been then, but tonight she didn't give a damn. There
was no agonising knot in her breast, no lump in her
throat. Not even the cool, cynical smile Peter Saxon had
given her when she'd opened the door to him could
pierce her armour.

'Miss Mitchell,' he'd said with a mocking bow, and

he'd handed her a nosegay of flowers. Wild flowers, she'd noticed, beautiful and perfect, and even as she shook her head in rejection she'd wondered where he'd managed to find them in the dead of winter.

'I don't want them, Mr Saxon,' she'd said curtly.

'Surely you wouldn't condemn them to death, Miss Mitchell,' he'd said, laughter in his voice.

Sara had said nothing, and finally he'd shrugged and dropped the little bouquet into the snow, where it lay like a crimson and blue stain.

'It doesn't matter,' he'd said carelessly. 'They don't match your dress, anyway.'

'No,' she'd said sharply. 'You didn't really think I would wear blue, did you?'

His smile had been almost weary. 'No,' he had said softly, 'I suppose I didn't.'

They had said little after that, but then, what would they have had to talk about? Peter Saxon had been impatient to reach the Winstead house. He'd checked the security systems that afternoon, Sara knew, but he said he wanted to make one last surveillance before the guests arrived.

She had watched as he checked the sensitivity parameters of the display cases in which the Maharanee of Gadjapur's jewels had been placed—whatever that meant—and then he'd checked the safe into which they would be put after midnight.

'OK', he muttered. 'The crash circuits are fine.'

That was meaningless to her, as well, but he had seemed satisfied. One last walk around the grounds, and then he'd nodded and pronounced everything ready.

The guests had begun arriving shortly afterwards, until finally the huge house was filled with laughter and music. And all evening Sara had dutifully followed Peter Saxon from room to room and guest to guest, watching as he kissed every perfumed cheek and smiled into every pair of long-lashed eyes and . . .

'You're so quiet, Miss Mitchell. Aren't you having a good time?'

Sara blinked and looked up at him. He was smiling that cool, cynical smile she had come to think of as his.

'I was wondering how much longer you planned on staying, Mr Saxon,' she said calmly. 'It's getting late. And your job is over, isn't it? The jewels have been back in the safe for two hours now.'

His smile grew even cooler. 'I thought we would stay until after they set dessert out, Miss Mitchell. Surely you can understand that?'

'No,' she said, 'I can't. I'm not interested in dessert. I——'

'But I am. How else will I be able to steal some tea-spoons to add to the knives and forks I stole earlier?'

Sara's chin lifted. 'I'm sure your sense of humour is much appreciated in some circles, Mr Saxon, but——'

'I'm staying until the party ends, Miss Mitchell. That's my job.' A smile tilted at the corner of his mouth. 'I'll call a taxi for you, if you like.'

'If you stay, I stay. As you say, that's my job.'

His eyes narrowed. 'Fine. When the evening ends, you can check my pockets.'

'Your sarcasm doesn't mean a thing to me, Mr Saxon. This wasn't my idea, remember? I'm as uncomfortable as you are, believe me.'

His eyes moved over her slowly, and then came back to her face. 'Oh, I do, Miss Mitchell. You sure as hell look uncomfortable in that dress. How can you breathe with those buttons closed all the way up to your chin?'

A flush spread over her cheeks. 'That's not what I meant, and you know it!'

'And since you raised the subject of what you're

wearing——'

'I did no such thing, Mr Saxon. You——'

'I thought I told you to wear something blue. Don't tell me a woman with eyes like yours doesn't own a blue dress.'

He was laughing at her, damn him! She could hear it in his voice, see it in his eyes. Sara drew a breath.

'What I wear is none of your business. I——'

He touched his hand to her cheek. 'The woman I'm with is always my business, Miss Mitchell.'

Sara felt her flush deepen. 'Stop it,' she hissed.

His teeth flashed. 'Easy, sweetheart. You're liable to draw attention to yourself, and you know you don't want to do that.'

'You don't know anything about what I want or don't want, Mr Saxon. You——'

'You would fade into the wallpaper if you could, Sara. That's why you wear your hair in that awful knot, why you wear dresses that look as if your grandmother chose them.'

Sara smiled coldly. 'Thievery and cheap psychiatry,' she said sweetly. 'A man of many talents. How nice.'

Peter Saxon grinned. 'That's the thing that fascinates me about you, Sara. Here we have this icy exterior——'

'If you think you can insult me, Mr Saxon——'

'. . . and beneath it there's a smouldering fire, just waiting to blaze.' His hand closed around her wrist. 'I keep thinking it might be interesting to be around when it happens.'

The touch of his hand made her heart hammer. What was the matter with her?

'Thievery, cheap psychiatry, and an over-active imagination,' she said evenly. 'I'm sure there are women who find the combination intriguing.'

His fingers moved against her skin. 'But not you,

of course.'

She shook her head. 'No, not me. I find you overbearing, insulting, irritating——'

He laughed softly. 'Stop trying to sweet-talk me, Sara. I'm here on business, and nothing you can do will take my mind off my work.'

Sara's eyebrows rose. 'Work, indeed, Mr Saxon. I hope General Casualty doesn't pay you much money for what you do.'

Peter sighed dramatically. 'Believe me, Sara, they don't pay me anywhere near what they should. If a man were bent on larceny, tonight would be worth a cool two or three million.'

'If you stole the Maharanee of Gadjapur's jewels, you mean?' She looked up at him as he drew her along beside him through the crowd. 'I'd think a pro like you would get the value right. They're worth five million, the paper said.'

Peter laughed as he took two flutes of champagne from a waiter. 'Retail,' he said, holding a glass out to her. 'Wholesale's different.'

Sara took the glass without thinking. 'Wholesale?'

'Jewels have to be fenced, Sara. You don't just take a handful, then walk into Tiffany's and offer them up for sale.' He looked at her and smiled. 'Still, a couple of million bucks isn't bad for a night's work.'

'A night's work,' she repeated flatly. 'That's a strange way to describe something so—so criminal.'

Peter grinned. 'See that little man in the corner? The fat one, with his arm around the tall blonde? I haven't heard what he does called "criminal".'

Sara looked across the room. The man in question was not just fat, he was oily-looking. Her pulse leaped.

'You mean, you recognise him? From—from prison? Is he here to try and steal the jewels?'

Peter sighed and shook his head. 'You've got a one-track mind, Miss Mitchell. No, of course not. He's a famous industrialist. He owns the controlling stock in one of the world's largest munitions' manufacturers. But he's not a crook, is he?'

'Now you're playing games, Mr Saxon. What he does is legal. What you do——'

He smiled thinly. 'I paid my debt to society. I'm a reformed thief, remember?'

'You don't sound like you're reformed at all. You sound as if you don't really believe theft is against the law.'

Peter shrugged. 'That's what they tell me.'

Sara stared at him. 'What they tell you? Don't you think that taking what isn't yours is wrong?'

He gave her a lazy smile. 'There are times you see something, Sara, and you know in your gut that it has only been waiting for you to come along and take it.' His eyes met hers, and a flame leaped to sudden life within their brown depths. 'Only a fool would walk away when that happens.'

Hell! Her knees were shaking. What was wrong with her? She knew what he was doing. He was having fun at her expense.

'Mr Saxon,' she said carefully, 'I wish you would——'

'Do you address all your dates so formally, Sara?'

Don't let him do this to you. He's playing with you the way a cat plays with a mouse, and it's up to you to stop him.

'Mr Saxon,' she repeated, 'it's very late. I'd appreciate it if you would help me find Chief Garrett. Tomorrow's a working day for me. Perhaps he'd agree to—to spend the rest of the evening with you, so I can call a taxi and——'

'Sara.' His voice was soft, as was his smile. He took her untouched champagne from her and set both flutes down on a table. 'Has it really been so terrible? Spending the evening with me, I mean.'

'I haven't spent the evening with you,' she said, before she could think of how the words would sound.

Peter smiled and took her hand in his. 'You're right. I've neglected you, Sara. And I apologise.'

'I didn't mean it like that,' she said quickly, trying not to feel the heat of his fingers against hers. 'This is . . . it's business.'

'Soft music. Flowers everywhere. A magnificent house and a spectacular view.' He laughed softly. 'Is your business day usually like this?'

She stiffened. What new game was this? What new embarrassment was he planning for her? She looked up at him warily, but the cynical smile was gone. He was looking at her with an unreadable expression on his face—one she found very disconcerting.

'I don't care what you think,' she said.

'You've passed up the lobster and caviare, you haven't had a sip of wine. It's obvious you don't like the people you've seen . . .'

'I'm not here for any of that, Mr Saxon. I——'

'. . . and you don't approve of me, or the way I earn my living.'

She looked at him as if he were insane. 'Approve of you? Approve of someone who cheats and steals——'

Peter sighed dramatically. 'That's what everyone says about insurance agents. That they steal from widows and orphans.'

'Insurance agents? But I wasn't referring to ins——'

'I mean, people approve of dentists and accountants. But not insurance agents. They tell jokes about us.

They say we're stodgy.'

'Mr Saxon, I wasn't referring to——'

He sighed again. 'What the hell, Miss Mitchell? I just happened to have some expertise in an insurance-related field. You wouldn't hold that against me, would you?'

Despite herself, a smile twitched at the corners of Sara's mouth. 'Mr Saxon, you know what I meant. I——'

'Forgive me for asking, Miss Mitchell, but might I interest you in a policy? Is your house properly insured? Your car? What about that damned cat of yours that tried to rub itself bald against my leg?'

She had to smile; she couldn't help it. She'd seen what had happened, although she hadn't said anything. In the moment it had taken Sara to get her coat, Taj had managed to deposit a lot of grey fur on Peter's black-gabardine-covered leg. At the time, it had seemed the least he deserved.

'I'm sorry about that,' she said. 'Taj doesn't get to see many strangers. He——'

'Strangers or strange men?'

'Neither. I don't——'

The unexpected admission caught in Sara's throat, but it was too late. She swallowed hard, then raised her eyes almost defiantly, waiting for Peter Saxon to make some jesting remark.

Her breath caught. He was looking at her as he had earlier in the day, as he had when he'd kissed her. Her heart skidded, then began to race.

'Mr Saxon——'

'Peter.'

'Mr Saxon, please . . .'

He smiled into her eyes. 'Peter.'

Sara swallowed again. 'Peter. I'd be grateful if

you'd——'

'Take you home. Yes, I know. And I shall, as soon as the party ends.'

'No. I . . . I can't stay any longer. I just . . . A cab would be fine. Really . . .'

He smiled again. 'You're supposed to stay with me, Sara. Remember? Those were your instructions. Chief Garrett wouldn't——'

Suddenly, the room was plunged into darkness. A collective sigh arose from the guests, there was a nervous giggle, and then the lights came on again.

'It's the storm, folks.' Simon Winstead stood in the doorway, a reassuring smile on his broad face. 'Don't worry about a thing. We've got lots of candles and lots of champagne. If one doesn't solve the problem, the other will.'

Appreciative laughter and a light smattering of applause greeted the announcement. Beside her, Peter muttered something under his breath.

'The fool would be better off if he told everybody to go home,' he said. 'The roads will be hell soon.'

Sara nodded. 'Yes, it's going to be almost impossible to get down the mountain. You would think he'd know that.'

Peter shrugged his shoulders. 'He knows it. But this is a big event for him. You don't expect something like a little common sense to intrude on his plans for tonight, do you?'

'Why don't you talk to him? Maybe he'd listen to you.'

'Winstead? Not very likely.'

'Yes, but suppose you told him how hard it would be for police cars to get here if there were some kind of trouble? That would impress him, wouldn't it?'

Peter cocked his head to the side. 'Well,' he said

softly, 'at least you don't try and hide that quick mind of yours.' He smiled, and his fingers threaded through hers. 'I'll make a deal with you, Sara. You dance with me, and I'll tell Winstead to shut down for the night. How does that sound?'

Dangerous. The answer came to her so quickly that she thought, at first, she'd said it aloud. But she hadn't; Peter was still smiling at her, waiting for her response.

'That's—that's silly. Why not just tell him now? Find him and——'

'You're wasting time, Sara. While we stand here arguing, the road's icing over.'

'Then what's the point in——?'

'One dance, Sara.' He slipped his arm around her waist and began walking her towards the adjoining greenhouse, where the indoor pool had been covered with a parquet dance-floor. 'What have you got to lose?'

'I . . . I'm not a very good dancer,' Sara said. 'I——'

The music reached out to them from the greenhouse. It was warm here, moist and fragrant with the breath of hundreds of orchids and frangipani. The lights were dim; she could see through the glass walls to where the snow lay like moonlight on the mountainside.

Peter drew Sara into his arms and smiled into her eyes.

'Just relax,' he said softly. 'Let yourself feel the music.'

'I told you, I'm not very good at this. I——'

His arms tightened around her. 'Let *me* be the judge of that, Sara.'

She knew she was moving stiffly within his arms. She had told him the truth—she'd never been much for

dancing. When she was thirteen, she'd closed the door
to her bedroom, turned the radio on low, and practised
the dances she'd seen in the movies. But there had never
been a chance to put her self-learned steps into practice,
except once in a great while at a wedding or a party.

The last time she'd danced was two years ago, at the
Garretts' twenty-fifth anniversary party. It was the
last time she'd worn this dress, too. It was an unbecom-
ing dress—she'd known it when she bought it. She still
remembered that day, how she had stood in Macy's,
looking at a blue chiffon dress with a low neckline
and full skirt, longing to try it on, but knowing it
was foolish to want something so frivolous.

She'd had a good time at the Garrett party. They
treated her as if she were family, and she felt at ease
with them. She'd danced more that night than she had
in years, with Jim and the men she worked with—even
with Jim's uncle, a white-haired old gentleman who
smelled of oil of wintergreen.

Sara inhaled and drew in Peter Saxon's scent. He
smelled of snow and heat, of champagne and the night.
It was a heady combination, and very, very male.
Her heart stumbled; her feet did, too, and his arms
tightened around her.

Feel the music, he'd said, but what she felt was the
strength of the arms that held her, the heat of the body
pressed to hers. What she felt was that same, sweet
weakness she'd felt this morning, when he had taken her
into his arms and kissed her.

'Sara.'

His voice was a soft caress in the shadowed room.
Sara closed her eyes and willed her heartbeat to slow,
her body to cease the sudden trembling that had seized
it.

'Sara.'

He wanted her to look at him. She could hear the unspoken command. But she couldn't look at him. She couldn't. If she did—if she did . . .

'Look at me,' he demanded.

'No,' she whispered.

He put his hand under her chin, and lifted her face to his. She drew in her breath as he bent his head and brushed his lips lightly over her mouth. She felt the bristling caress of his moustache, the heat of his breath. He whispered her name, and his hands spread on her back, the fingers of one splaying over her hips to her buttocks.

'Please,' she sighed, 'oh, please . . .'

He drew her close against him, and she felt the hungry message of his body against hers.

'Sara,' he murmured, 'sweet Sara.'

'Please . . .' she said, although she no longer knew what it was that she was pleading for.

Peter kissed her again, his mouth moving over hers. She felt the touch of his tongue on her lips, and a flame sprang to life deep within her. Her hands touched his chest, moved up his shoulders to his neck; her lips parted beneath his.

Suddenly, he clasped her shoulders and held her away from him. She swayed as she opened her eyes and focused blindly on his face. He smiled, and put his hand against her cheek.

'The lights,' he said softly.

Sara blinked. The lights. Of course. They had gone out again. And this time they hadn't come back on.

'The storm's getting worse,' he whispered. 'Wait here for me while I find Winstead and tell him the party's over.' He bent to her, and brushed his mouth over hers. 'Then I'll take you home, sweet Sara.'

The husky promise in his voice sent a tremor through her. 'I'll go with you,' she said. 'Peter——'

He laughed softly. 'Like this?' His hands touched her hair, her lips, and she realised suddenly how she must look. Her hair had come loose from its clasp, and lay in silken disarray on her shoulders. And her lips were swollen, hot with his kisses.

'I won't be long.' He cupped her face in his hands and lifted it to his. 'Will you wait for me, sweet Sara?'

Sara ran her tongue across her lips. She felt as if one of her dreams had come to life, and she were living a fantasy. She looked into Peter Saxon's eyes and nodded shyly.

'Yes,' she breathed. 'I'll wait.'

His teeth flashed whitely in the dark room. 'Give me five minutes.'

She watched as he turned and hurried through the greenhouse. Matches flared in the darkness; she saw the flicker of candles, heard the murmur of voices, but every fibre of her being was concentrated on Peter's retreating figure. Five minutes, he'd said. Five minutes, and then he would take her home.

Her mouth went dry. There was no pretending she didn't know what he had meant by that. He was going to make love to her. His kisses, his hands, everything he'd done had carried the message. He would stay with her tonight, and then . . .

Sara put her hand to her mouth. What a fool she'd been! 'I've never taken anything from a woman that she didn't offer gladly'—wasn't that what he had said when she'd taunted him this morning? Peter Saxon had tried every way possible to humiliate her, and moments ago he had finally found the one that worked.

Quickly, cloaked by the darkness, Sara hurried through the greenhouse towards the little room just off the foyer where she'd left her coat. Tears of anger rose in her eyes, and she brushed them away.

It was a pity she could never tell her boss the truth, she thought, as she pulled on her coat and hurried to the front door. He had been worried about Peter Saxon stealing the Maharanee's jewels, but it wasn't the jewels Peter Saxon had been after tonight.

The jewels were much too well-protected. Wasn't it unfortunate that she couldn't say the same thing about herself?

CHAPTER THREE

SARA stepped through the front door and slammed it shut behind her. Snow, driven by a cold wind, stung her cheeks and eyes, but she paid no attention to it. Anger burned within her like a flame, directed as much at herself as at Peter Saxon.

How could she have been so stupid? To think she'd let someone like that make a fool of her—to think that she'd . . . she'd almost . . .

But she hadn't. That was what counted. If only she could step back into the house for a minute—just long enough to see his face when he came hurrying back to the greenhouse and realised his naïve little conquest had fled the trap. She could at least imagine it, and that was almost satisfaction enough. That was . . .

A sudden gust of wind drove into her with such force, it almost took her breath away. Sara pulled her gloves from her pockets, and pulled them on her already numb hands. Lord, but it was freezing! And the snow was falling so heavily that she could hardly see past the end of her nose. Hank and Tommy had been at work—the long, circular driveway had been recently ploughed and sanded—but at this rate the snow would soon obliterate their efforts.

Sara drew up her coat-collar, then carefully made her way down the wide brick steps to the driveway. Cars hulked its length like silent, white-coated beasts.

She took a tentative step forward, and clutched wildly at the air as her feet almost slid out from under her. Terrific! The packed snow was as slippery as glass. But

41

there was nowhere else to walk—on the unploughed lawn, the snow lay in knee-high drifts.

Now what, Sara? she berated herself. You don't really think you can walk down the mountain, do you?

No. Not in these thin-soled, high-heeled shoes; not on a night like this. She looked over her shoulder at the Winstead house. The windows were alive with the soft glow of candlelight. It looked warm and inviting, but she wasn't about to go inside. When Peter Saxon saw her, that damned cynical smile of his would turn to insolent laughter. He would probably say something witty that would make a fool of her in front of everybody—if she hadn't already done that herself. She didn't even want to think about how many people had probably seen the way she'd behaved on the dance-floor.

And just why did you act that way, Sara? You never have before.

Impatiently, she pushed the thought aside, and burrowed deeper into her coat. What mattered now was finding a way down the mountain. She could always wait out here for Jim and Alice to leave.

You could always wait out here and turn blue.

There had to be another choice. There had to be some other way.

Far down the long driveway a car engine coughed, then roared to life. Headlights blinked in the darkness, and a dark shape began to move slowly towards the distant gate.

Sara took a step forward, then another. 'Hey . . . hey, wait!' She broke into an awkward run, trying not to fall, waving her hands over her head in a desperate bid for the driver's attention. But the car picked up speed, slid gently as it negotiated a long curve, and was swallowed up by the falling snow.

Her breath puffed whitely as she tottered along the drive. There was still a good chance she could catch the car. It would have to slow when it reached the gate—there was a hairpin turn just past it that would be impossible to negotiate at speed on a night such as this. The electronic gate itself had been left open, so that party-goers could come and go with ease. Peter Saxon had grumbled about how poor an idea that was, while they had waited for the guard who was checking invitations to pass them through.

Yes, she could see the car now. The gate was just ahead, and the car was slowing as it eased into the turn.

'Wait. Please wait!'

Sara ran faster, but not fast enough. And there was no way the occupants would hear her with the windows closed and the defroster going. Her footsteps slowed, and she finally stumbled to a halt, watching helplessly as the vehicle reached a straight stretch of road and picked up speed. The tail-lights winked in the dark, and then they were gone.

Silence, punctuated only by the moan of the wind and the rasp of her own breath, settled around her. Sara peered over her shoulder. The house was somewhere far behind her, invisible in the storm. She would have to walk back, much as she hated the thought. But there was no choice. The snow was . . .

Headlights materialised in the darkness, glowing like the great eyes of a jungle-cat. Another car was coming, this one moving far too rapidly for the icy road. But she could stop it. All she had to do was step in front of the lights.

The car skidded as the driver slammed on the brakes. The sound of the tyres vainly trying to grip the icy surface was a sibilant hiss. She watched, horrified, as the rear end began to fish-tail in lazy arcs. An eternity seemed to pass until, finally, the car came to a stop diagonally across the road.

Sara lifted her skirt and ran towards it, as the driver's door opened and a figure stepped out.

'Are you all right?' she asked. 'I didn't mean to——'

The words caught in her throat. Peter Saxon stood before her, glaring at her in fury.

'What kind of stupid stunt was that? Were you trying to kill us both?'

Sara stared at him. 'What are you doing here?'

'I think I'm the one who's supposed to ask that question, Miss Mitchell.'

Her chin lifted. 'What does it look like I'm doing? I'm—I'm walking. I——'

'Walking,' he said in an expressionless voice.

'That's right. So if you'll just——'

'Get in the car, Miss Mitchell.'

She shook her head. 'Thanks, but I'd rather—hey! Hey, what do you think you're doing? Let go of me. Did you hear wh——'

'Get in the car,' he said through his teeth. His hand tightened on hers as he pulled her towards the passenger door.

'No, I certainly will not. I——'

Her protests were useless. Peter yanked the door open and shoved her into the seat. A second later, he was seated beside her.

'Buckle your seat-belt,' he ordered.

Sara reached for the door-handle, and his hand closed around her wrist. Pinpoints of light glowed in his eyes as he looked at her. When he spoke again, his voice was soft and cold.

'If I were you, Miss Mitchell, I wouldn't do anything to provoke me.'

She stared at him, and then she sank back against the seat.

'Good girl,' he said. 'Now, go on—buckle your belt.'

'I don't need you to tell me what to do,' Sara said, the bravado of her words a screen for the sudden fear beating in her blood.

The car shot forward. 'Well, then, use your head,' he said unpleasantly. 'I just don't want you killed if we skid off this mountain.' He looked over at her, and his teeth flashed in the darkness. 'I'm saving that pleasure for myself.'

The light from the car's dashboard had joined with the snow's reflection to cast an eerie illumination on his face. She could see the gleam of his eyes, the narrowed hardness of his mouth, the tic of a muscle high in his cheek.

'That was a neat bit of fancy footwork you pulled, Miss Mitchell.'

It was safer to deliberately misunderstand him. 'If you hadn't been driving so quickly——' she began, and he laughed coldly.

'Please, let's not waste each other's time. You know damned well what I'm talking about.'

'Listen, Mr Saxon, I don't have to explain——'

'I spent a hell of a lot of time peering into corners, asking people if they had seen you, before I figured out that you'd conned me.'

'A charming choice of words,' Sara said. It was amazing, she thought, that her voice could sound so cool and calm, even while her heart threatened to leap out from under her ribs.

'Is that why you set me up? To teach a lesson to an ex-con?'

'I told you, I don't have to explain myself to——'

'I wouldn't have thought a woman like you would

make a fool out of a man.'

A woman like you. Yes, she was right about him. He'd been playing with her all the time. But two could play at that game.

'It wasn't difficult,' she said. 'You didn't need much help at all.'

For a moment, she thought she'd pushed him too far. His head swung towards her, and the coldness in his eyes made the chill of the winter night seem warm. Then he looked back at the road and laughed.

'You've got guts, Sara. I'll give you that much.' He leaned forward and wiped his hand over the rear-view mirror. 'Just where were you going when you walked out of the house?'

She looked at him, and then stared straight ahead. 'Home.'

'So you decided to sneak out of the door——'

'I didn't sneak out of the door. I simply——'

'You skulked out of the house so you could hike a mile down Stone Mountain in the middle of a blizzard. That was really very clever.' His voice was thick with sarcasm. 'Hell, with a little luck you would have frozen to death and *really* done a number on me. I can see the headline now: "Con Kills Cutie". That would sell a million papers!'

'You're talking nonsense,' Sara said sharply. 'Nothing would have happened to me. I know this mountain——'

'. . . and you always walk it in the dark, in the midst of a storm, with your skirts dragging in the snow and your shoes frozen to your feet. Yes, I'm sure.'

Sara shifted uncomfortably. Her feet *were* like lumps of ice. And the wet hem of her dress was sticking to her legs. The car's heater was on, but she was shivering anyway. However, if Peter Saxon expected her to thank him . . .

'I'd have gotten a ride,' she said stubbornly. 'After all, the party's over.'

The car slowed as they neared the foot of the mountain. 'Not by a long shot, it isn't. That damned fool Winstead says he won't call it a night until the champagne's all gone.' He peered into the swirling snow as they reached the road's intersection with the highway, then accelerated. The car skidded delicately, then shot forward into the night. 'Which means they'll still be partying some time tomorrow.'

Sara looked at him. 'And you left anyway? I thought you said you would stay until the party ended.'

He glanced at her, and then at the road. 'There was no point,' he said curtly.

'Yes, but——'

'Which exit do we take to your house, Sara? The one coming up or the next?'

'The next,' she said. 'But what about the jewels?'

He laughed. 'Stop worrying about them. Believe me, they're fine.'

'I'm sure they are. I just don't understand why you said——'

The shrill wail of a siren cut through the night. Lights flashed in the oncoming lane, and a state police cruiser sped past them. Sara twisted around in her seat, staring after the car as it vanished into the darkness.

'I wonder what that's all about?' she said slowly.

Peter glanced in the rear-view mirror. 'There's probably an accident behind us somewhere. There'll be a dozen before the night's over.'

She nodded. 'I suppose so. This is a bad road under the best of conditions, and——'

Lights flashed ahead of them again. This time, a pair of police cars flew past, their tyres spewing snow and ice as they skidded through a curve. Sara peered over her shoulder and watched them until they disappeared.

'Do you think they went up Stone Mountain Road?'

'If they did, it's because some fool went off that curve at the gate.'

Sara looked at him. 'The jewels——'

'The jewels are fine. If you want to worry about something, worry about this road.'

'Yes, but——'

Peter's voice was harsh. 'Dammit, Sara, I could use another pair of eyes.'

'You're taking this awfully calmly, aren't you? Those jewels are your responsibility. I should think——'

'You're letting your imagination run wild, Sara. Besides, they're the museum's responsibility now. Their representative is satisfied with the arrangements.' He glanced at her and then at the road. 'For heaven's sake, relax! The safe won't even be opened until the jewels are transferred to the museum for exhibit.'

Sara shook her head. 'I just don't understand you at all,' she said. 'This morning——'

A dark shape bolted from the brush and streaked across the road.

'Hang on!' Peter yelled, and he spun the wheel hard to the right.

The car floated gracefully across the icy road, the tyres spinning uselessly against the frozen surface. Trees loomed darkly through the heavy snowfall; there was the blare of a horn as a truck sped by them. Sara watched in stunned silence as Peter struggled to bring the car under control. Finally, with a crunch, it lurched heavily on to the verge of the road, then came to a shuddering halt.

'Hell,' Peter whispered. Quickly, he unfastened his seat-belt and swivelled towards Sara. 'Are you all right?

Sara?'

She nodded and took a deep breath. 'Yes,' she whispered. 'Fine. I . . . What was that in the road? Did we hit it?'

'A dog. Or a fox, maybe. I think we missed it.' He laughed shakily. 'I hope the little beggar appreciates the sacrifice we almost made. That was one hell of a skid. We hit the shoulder pretty hard.' He wrenched open the door, and a blast of frigid air swept into the car. 'I'd better check and make sure we didn't blow a tyre.'

Sara fumbled to unfasten her belt. 'I'll get out, too. I can look for whatever ran across the road.'

Peter shook his head. 'I'll do it. You stay put. There's no sense in both of us freezing our tails off.'

The door closed after him. Sara shuddered, and dug her hands deep into her coat pockets. What a close call that had been! It was nice to know Peter was the kind of man who would . . .

She laughed and leaned her head back against the seat. He was the kind of man who stole for a living. He was the kind of man who thought nothing of playing with a woman, of making her look foolish and stupid. Anyone would try to avoid an animal in the road. That didn't prove anything at all.

She turned in her seat, watching as he walked slowly back along the road, checking it carefully, until finally the falling snow swallowed him up. When he reappeared, he was shaking his head.

'Nothing here!' he yelled, his voice barely audible through the wound-up windows.

Peter bent down, and she knew he was looking at the rear tyres. After a few minutes, he walked to the front of the car. There was a thudding sound—he was kicking the tyre, Sara thought—and then he straightened and walked towards her. She wound her window down a bit, and looked up at him.

'The damned tyre's flat. I'll have to change it.'

She wound the window down a little further. His hair was wind-tossed and covered with snow; his nose and cheeks were red.

'Is there anything I can do to help?'

He shook his head. 'Nothing.' He gave her a quick smile. 'Just stay in the car, and keep warm for both of us.'

'Don't be silly. You have to jack the car up. I'll get out so that——'

'Stay put, Sara. It's as cold as the North Pole out here.' He pulled off his gloves, stuffed them into his pockets, and smiled again.

'Peter, that's crazy. I——'

His smile fled, and his voice grew harsh. 'Dammit, Sara, don't argue with me! Just stay where you are.'

Colour flared in her cheeks, and she wound the window up again. All right, let him play at being Superman! If he wanted to stand out there all alone and freeze, who was she to complain?

He moved to the back of the car and she heard the boot open. The car bounced as he leaned on it. She drew up her collar, then reached out and switched on the radio. Music wailed into the silence, and she switched from station to station until she heard the drone of an announcer's voice.

'. . . eight inches already on the ground, and at least another four predicted. Winds from the west, clocking in at thirty miles per hour. The best advice we can offer is to stay at home. Driving conditions are very bad and worsening. Visibility is poor . . .'

Poor wasn't the half of it, Sara thought. She remembered how quickly Peter had faded from sight as he'd walked away from the car moments ago. If a car

or a truck came along . . . They were parked on the
verge, yes, but that didn't mean anything. How many
times over the years had she dispatched Jack Barnes's
tow-truck to the highway, to pick up what was left of a
car that had been smashed to pieces while it was 'safely'
parked on the shoulder?

Sara craned her neck and looked behind her. The
boot was still up, and she couldn't see anything. Did
Peter keep flares in his tool-kit? she wondered. Not
many drivers carried them. But most had a flashlight. If
she could find one, it would make sense to stand behind
the car with it, so she could warn off oncoming traffic.

She leaned forward and opened the glove compart-
ment. Maps. Loose coins. A pencil. And—yes, a flashlight.

She flicked the switch with her thumb, and a narrow
beam of light swept through the car. It wasn't as bright
as it might have been, but it would have to do. Quickly,
she opened the door and stepped out.

Snow blew into her face, the flakes knife-sharp and
cold. Sara ducked her head against the wind as she
hurried towards the rear of the car. No, he hadn't set
out flares. He hadn't done anything, in fact. He was
simply standing there, leaning into the open boot.

Sara switched the flashlight on, and aimed it at him.
His head came up sharply, and he sprang away from the
boot.

'I thought I told you——'

'You did.' She gave him a hesitant smile. After all,
she thought, if it weren't for him, she might still be
standing in the snow on top of Stone Mountain. 'But I
thought it would be a good idea if——'

Her hurried explanation broke off as the light shone
on Peter's face. Sara saw his narrowed eyes, his down-
turned mouth, even the muscle moving in his cheek.

'Turn that damned thing off,' he snarled.

She gaped at him in surprise. The light swung in an arc as she pointed it away from his face.

'I'm sorry,' she said. 'I was only trying——'

Everything seemed to happen at once. The car door swung wide—the wind, she thought hazily—and the dispassionate voice from the radio overrode hers.

'. . . theft of the fabulous jewels of the Maharanee of Gadjapur. State police report that the daring robbery was the work of Peter Saxon, the society cat burglar . . .'

Sara drew in her breath. 'What's he talking about? The jewels——'

Peter held out his hand. 'Give me the flashlight,' he said quietly.

She looked up at him. 'Didn't you hear that news report? It said——'

'The flashlight, Sara.'

His hand closed around hers, as cold and hard as his voice. Sara tried to jerk free, and the narrow beam of light danced in the dimly lit boot. Suddenly, it fell on an open tool-box, and a thousand tiny suns blazed to life.

'Oh, no!'

Her words drifted into the silent night. Sara stared at the incredible tumble of jewels that had been caught in the wavering beam of the flashlight. Emeralds, diamonds, sapphires, rubies . . .

'The Maharanee's jewels,' she whispered. She forced her eyes from the tool-box to Peter Saxon's face. 'You stole them. You——'

He slammed the boot shut, took the flashlight from her nerveless fingers and switched it off. Darkness settled around them.

'If only you had listened to me, Sara,' he said softly.

There was an undercurrent in his voice that chilled her

far more than the wind and the steadily falling snow.
She took a step back.

'What—what are you going to do?'

'I asked you to stay in the car, didn't I?'

'No. Don't——'

She struck out at him as he reached for her, but he
brushed her hands away. His arm clamped around her
waist like steel. Then, half lifting her from her feet, he
drew her to the car and shoved her inside.

'I'm going to change the tyre,' he said softly. His face
was almost against hers; Sara felt the warmth of his
breath on her skin. 'You're not to move while I'm doing
it.'

'You can't do this,' she whispered. 'You can't——'

His hand closed on her jaw, and he forced her face to
his. 'Do you understand me, Sara? If you try and
run . . .'

The unspoken threat hung in the air between them.
Sara's heart skipped erratically.

'What—what are you going to do with me?'

A smile twisted across his mouth. 'I'll think of
something,' he said.

He looked into her eyes. Terror twisted through her;
she knew what he was going to do just before he bent to
her, but there was nothing she could do to stop him. His
fingers were like steel clamps on her jaw.

'No,' she whimpered, and then his mouth was on
hers, his kiss swift and passionate. Something darker
and more powerful than fear swept through her, and she
made a quick, soft sound deep in her throat.

Peter lifted his head, and ran his thumb lightly
across her parted lips. He looked down at her, his
expression unreadable.

'I promise, sweet Sara,' he whispered, 'I'll think of
something.'

His hand fell away from her, and he stepped back into the darkness.

CHAPTER FOUR

THE CAR moved swiftly through the dark night, the heavy silence broken only by the rush of heated air from the defroster and the sibilant hiss of the windscreen wipers, as they struggled against the steady snowfall. Sara looked at the speedometer. The needle stood at fifty, much too fast for the icy road conditions. Peter Saxon had to know that: the skid that had sent them spinning off the road, that had led to her seeing the fortune inside the boot of his car, was all the warning he should have needed.

Sara's glance flew to his face, then away. In the glow of the dashboard, his profile was implacable. He looked, she thought, cold and dangerous and cunning.

A knot of fear lodged in her throat. It was difficult to swallow, much less to breathe. The man beside her was a criminal, far stronger than she. And she was at his mercy, trapped in a nightmare with no end in sight. What did Peter Saxon want of her? It was the single thought that tormented her as the minutes passed.

I'll find something to do with you, sweet Sara.

A tremor raced along her skin, and she shuddered. No. He wasn't like that. Even after his arrest, two years before, when the newspapers had been filled with columns about the man they had dubbed the 'Thief of Hearts', there had never been even the suggestion that he used violence. His victims were always away or asleep when he stole from them—and it was always jewels he'd stolen, nothing else.

I never took anything from a woman that she didn't

offer gladly.

She took another quick look at him. No, she thought, a man like Peter Saxon wouldn't have to force himself on a woman. His rugged good looks and the aura of danger that surrounded him were a magnetic combination.

Sara bit down on her lip and stared ahead of her. But the situation was different this time. He wasn't a cat burglar in a darkened bedroom, and she wasn't a society beauty asleep in her bed. She was the woman who had spoiled his plans. He'd pulled off an incredible theft, and she had ruined it.

If only she hadn't got out of the car. If only she hadn't pointed the flashlight at the boot. If only . . .

'How much money do you have with you, Sara?'

His voice startled her as it cut through the silence she'd wrapped around herself.

'Money?'

'That's what I said. How much do you have?'

She fumbled her bag open, and peered into her purse. 'Twenty—no, thirty dollars.'

His eyes went to the rear-view mirror, then to the road ahead. 'Is there a branch of Federated of New York anywhere around here?'

'The bank? Yes, in the next town. But——'

'How do I get there?'

Money. Of course, he needed money to get away.

Her hands shook as she opened her wallet and pulled out the bills. 'You can have my thirty dollars,' she said, holding the banknotes out to him. 'And I have credit cards. Visa. MasterCard. Take them. I——'

'And do what with them? Do *I* look like Sara Mitchell?'

She stared at the cards in her hand. 'There must be a way——'

'I have my own cards. They're useless—unless I want to tell people who I am and where I am.' He glanced at her, and a cold smile curved across his mouth. 'Or was that what you were hoping, sweet Sara?'

'No,' she said quickly, 'I never thought——'

'How many years have you worked for the police?' His eyes moved to the rear-view mirror, then to the road ahead. 'Long enough to know all the tricks, I bet.'

Sara shook her head. 'I wasn't thinking. Really. I was just trying to find a way to . . . to . . .'

'I spent sixteen months in prison,' he said roughly. 'Believe me, Sara, you learn a few tricks there, too.' He looked at her, then back at the road. 'And I promise you, I'm a damn sight better than you'll ever be.'

She ran her tongue over her lips. 'All I meant was that you could take my money and let me go.'

He laughed. 'Such a generous offer. Would you want me to drop you off at a phone booth, so you can call your boss and tell him where to find the jewels?'

'He already knows you have them, Mr Saxon. He——'

'He *assumes* I have them,' he interrupted curtly. 'And it's a hell of a long way from assumption to fact.'

'But you *do* have them,' Sara said, before she had time to think. 'They're in the boot. I saw them.'

The words were out before she could stop them. Peter Saxon laughed coldly.

'Exactly. *You* saw them, Sara. Only you.'

Icy fingers seemed to dance along her spine. 'What . . . what do you mean? You can't——'

'You and I are going on a little trip, Sara.' His head swivelled towards her; she saw the gleam of his teeth. 'A vacation, if you like. But we need some cash first—which brings me back to the question I asked you. Is there a branch of Federated of New York around here?'

A fear unlike any she had ever known wrapped its cold tendrils around her. *A trip.* 'You and I are going on a little trip.' Sara drew a long, shuddering breath.

'You're making a terrible mistake,' she said quickly. 'So far, all they want you for is theft. You——'

His leather-gloved fingers tightened on the wheel. 'Theft is enough,' he said grimly. 'Where the hell is that bank?'

'Please, just listen to me——'

His hand shot from the wheel to her lap, and he caught her wrist so tightly that she cried out.

'The bank, damn you! Where is it?'

Tears of pain and frustration rose in her eyes. 'Get out at the next exit,' she said stiffly. 'You'll see it on your right.'

The pressure of his hand eased. 'Thank you,' he said.

Sara didn't answer. She blinked back her tears and stared out of the window; after a second or two, he put his hand back on the steering wheel.

What was he going to do? she thought. Rob a bank? Why not? A man who would steal a fortune in gems and kidnap a woman wouldn't be choosy about where he got his money. The fact that he wanted a particular bank was an interesting touch. Did Federated use locks Peter Saxon could open more easily than others?

Manic laughter rose in her throat, and she forced it back. What was it Alice Garrett had said this afternoon? It had been something about the excitement of going to the biggest party of the year with a celebrity—and now, here she was, going to a bank with a robber. That had to rate even higher on the excitement scale. And to think—to think she'd planned to spend tonight reading, with Taj curled in her lap . . . The way you've spent every night for the past seven years, Sara. The way you'll spend the next fifty. Instead, you're racing into the night beside a man more exciting than any you've ever dreamed of.

She blinked in surprise. Was she going crazy? What kind of thinking was that? What kind of nonsense . . .?

The car skidded gently as they took the exit ramp. 'Is that it?' Peter Saxon asked, nodding towards a low glass and steel building barely visible through the curtain of snow.

'Yes.' Her voice was hoarse. 'Are you sure you want to do this, Mr Saxon? You'll just be adding crime to crime——'

He stared at her, and then he gave a short bark of laughter. 'I hate to disappoint you, Sara, but your imagination is working overtime. All I want to do is use their cash-machine with my bankcard.'

His bankcard. The terrible laughter bubbled up in her throat again and she swallowed past it. Of course! This was the age of the computer. Peter Saxon, ex-convict, jewel thief, kidnapper, wanted to make a withdrawal, but he didn't need a gun for that. All he needed was a thin plastic card.

The tyres squealed as he turned into the car park beside the deserted bank. The wind had swept across the open space, playfully depositing the snow in uneven drifts. The area nearest to the road was relatively clear, but the bank itself, and the looming cash-machine, were tucked behind a knee-high drift.

He pulled as close to the drift as he could, then switched off the lights and engine. The sudden silence and darkness seemed ominous.

'Listen carefully, Sara.' His voice was soft, but there was an undertone in it that made the hair rise on the back of her neck. He took the keys from the ignition, undid his seat-belt and moved closer to her. 'You're to sit perfectly still and wait for me. Do you understand?'

'They're probably looking for your car by now,' she said breathlessly. 'The state police will have your licence-plate number, and the local cops, and Chief Garrett——'

He pulled off his glove and put his hand lightly over her mouth. The heat of his skin felt like flame against her cool lips.

'It's a rental car, Sara. With luck, it will take Garrett a while to figure that out and trace it. By then, we'll be somewhere safe.' His hand lifted from her mouth, but stayed against her cheek. 'Don't waste your time hoping they'll catch me, Sara,' he said softly. 'It's not going to happen.'

She stared at him, while her mind spun in furious circles. It would be foolish to underestimate him. He'd planned all this—the theft, his escape, the 'somewhere safe'—the only thing he hadn't counted on was her seeing what lay in the boot of the car. Her part in it, she thought suddenly, was to have ended late tonight, in her bed. She would have been an unexpected bonus, the naïve, small-town spinster just ripe for the picking.

To a man like Peter Saxon, a man who lived on the edge, the risk of lingering for another few hours would have seemed minimal. It might even have added a sense of excitement to the theft. And there wasn't any reason to rush; no one was supposed to look at the jewels for another four days.

But something had gone wrong, something he hadn't planned on, that had led to the premature discovery of his crime. And now she was here, the unwilling captive of a man who would do whatever had to be done to make good his escape.

'Sara,' his thumb moved lightly over her lips, 'if you do as you're told, you'll be all right. Do you understand?'

She nodded. 'Yes,' she said, but it was a lie. She could hear it in her own voice, as he must have. His eyes grew dark, and his hand clasped her jaw.

'Don't make me do anything we'll both regret,' he whispered.

His mouth dropped to hers and he kissed her. Then, before she could catch her breath, he opened the door and stepped out of the car.

She watched as he ducked his head against the wind and started towards the drift that separated him from the cash-machine. Her heart was pounding erratically, and she put her hand to her lips, almost expecting to feel the heated imprint of his mouth against her fingertips.

Goodness, what was happening to her? Even in her terror, there had been a swift second of something else, some spiralling excitement that had thickened her blood.

Hadn't she once read that fear did strange things to people? Yes, there had been an article in some police magazine in the office. Clever criminals could manipulate ordinary citizens, the article had said, when those citizens were caught in situations over which they had no control.

Sara drew a deep breath. Of course. Peter Saxon was manipulating her. And she had reacted just as he'd expected.

She sat up straighter and stared after him. How long would it take him to get the money? He'd reached the machine, but he hadn't inserted his card yet. He was tucking his gloves into his pocket, taking out his wallet . . .

A minute to locate the card. Another to insert it and activate the machine, and then another to collect the money.

Three minutes. Four, if she were lucky. It wasn't

enough. But it was all the time she had.

Sara drew in her breath, willing her pounding heart to slow. Carefully, quietly, her eyes never leaving Peter Saxon, she eased the car door open. He had found his card, he was leaning towards the machine . . .

Now!

She exploded from the car in a swirl of wool coat and flaring silk skirt, her feet slipping on the icy ground.

'Sara!'

His voice came after her like a gunshot, sharp in the cold air. She drew in a desperate breath as she raced across the snow-covered car park. Adrenalin pumped through her veins; she felt her heart thudding in her chest, heard her breath rasp, tasted the metallic bite of urgency on her tongue.

The muffled pound of his footsteps was close behind her. A sob broke from her throat. If only a car would come by . . .

Not in the middle of the night, Sara. Not in the middle of a blizzard. Not in a million years of hoping.

She cried out as his arms went around her, and they slipped, stumbled, and went down together, landing heavily on the snowy ground in a tangle of limbs. Sara's leg twisted beneath her, taking both Peter Saxon's weight and hers.

They lay stunned for a second, the vapour of their breath mingling in the cold air, and then tears of frustration and anger welled in her eyes.

'Damn you!' she cried, striking out at him with her free hand. 'Damn you to hell!'

Peter Saxon caught hold of her wrist, then stood and pulled her roughly to her feet.

'What the hell kind of stunt was that?' he snarled.

The clip that held her hair had come loose when she'd fallen. Sara flung her snow-dampened hair back from her face, and stared at him defiantly.

'Did you really expect me to sit there and wait for you to come back?' she said.

He drew a deep breath, then let it out. 'No,' he said, and then his mouth narrowed. 'No,' he repeated, 'I suppose I didn't.' She winced as he forced her arm up behind her back. 'Now, move, damn it! We're wasting time.'

He started towards the car with Sara beside him. She flinched as she put her weight on her foot. The ankle hurt; she must have twisted it, she thought. Every step was painful. Her wrist and arm hurt, too. Peter Saxon's grip was like steel, and he was holding her arm at an almost impossible angle behind her. But she made no outcry—not even when he pushed her through the knee-high drift to the cash-machine. The snow was as cold as an ice bath, soaking through her long skirt and thin shoes almost immediately.

She was shaking with cold by the time he'd collected a stack of banknotes and shoved her into the car. She stared straight ahead while Peter Saxon got in beside her and shut his door.

'Did I hurt you?'

His voice was harsh. Sara looked down at her lap and found, to her surprise, that she was rubbing her wrist. The imprint of his fingers was vivid.

'Yes,' she said stiffly.

He reached past her and locked her door. His hand brushed lightly over her breasts.

'I can do worse than that, if you make me,' he said quietly. 'Remember that, Sara.' The engine coughed, then came to life, and he looked at her again. 'Are you cold?'

There was no point in denying the truth, not when her teeth were chattering like castanets. She nodded her

head. There was a second's silence, and then she heard
the rustle of fabric and his overcoat fell in her lap.

'Put that over you.'

'I don't want it,' she said, but he wasn't paying any
attention to her. She watched as he looked carefully into
his rear-view mirror, then into the deserted road.
Finally, he pressed the accelerator and the car slid into
the night.

She sat in silence, the coat bunched on her lap, as the
streets slipped by.

'There's no one to treat you for frostbite where we're
going,' he said after a while.

'I won't get frostbite.'

He shrugged. 'Pneumonia, then. There's no one to
treat that, either.'

Sara glanced at him. Was he laughing at her? It was
impossible to tell. But it didn't matter. The simple fact
was that she was cold—colder than she had ever been in
her life. He'd turned the heat up, and warm gusts of air
blew over her face and feet, but she was still shivering,
her teeth were still chattering, and the last thing she
needed was to get sick.

She spread his coat and tucked it around herself. It
covered her from chin to toe. She felt warmer right
away, and she sighed and settled more deeply into the
soft wool. It brushed her nose, and she smelled the
musky scent of wet wool along with the deeper tone of
Peter Saxon's own scent. She remembered the smell of
him as he'd held her in his arms. It was a clean smell, a
heady one . . .

She sat up quickly, and pulled the coat down to her
waist. Peter Saxon glanced over at her.

'Better?' She nodded, still not looking at him, and he
flexed his hands on the wheel. 'It's your own damned
fault you got soaked. If you had stayed put——'

He broke off, and his eyes went to the rear-view mirror. Sara's glance followed his, and her breath caught. There were lights coming up behind them. Headlights. Please, she thought, please, oh please . . .

But the car sped by them, and vanished into the snowy darkness ahead.

'Damned fool,' Peter Saxon growled. He glanced at the speedometer, then at the road. 'He's doing sixty, at least.'

Sara stared at him. 'And you're doing fifty. Much, much safer on a road like this, I'm sure.'

His lips drew back from his teeth. 'The limit's fifty-five. Even if some cop is foolish enough to be cruising this road tonight, he's not going to stop a car doing a respectable fifty miles per hour.'

'You've thought of everything, haven't you?'

He shrugged his shoulders. 'I hope so.'

Sara shifted in her seat. 'There's one thing you haven't thought of,' she said quickly. Peter Saxon looked at her, and she drew in her breath. 'You haven't thought of what will happen to you when they catch you.'

His mouth narrowed, and he looked back to the road. 'They won't.'

'Listen to me, Mr Saxon. All they want you for now is theft.'

His eyes moved swiftly to the rear-view mirror, then to the road. 'Keep quiet, Sara.'

His voice was curt. She knew it was meant as a warning, but she had gone too far to stop now.

'What's the sense in taking me with you?'

He laughed. 'How would I have found the Federated bank without you, Sara?'

'I'll only slow you down,' she said desperately. 'And what good will it do you? It's not as if I can tell anyone anything. I don't know what your plans are, or where you're going——'

'I'm going north,' he said bluntly. 'Towards the Adirondack Mountains.'

Sara shook her head. 'I don't want to hear it,' she said quickly. 'I can't tell the police anything if I don't know anything. And I don't. I——'

'And will you have selective amnesia about the jewels?'

She stared at him. 'I don't understand.'

'No,' he said through his teeth, 'no, you certainly don't. Which is why, sweet Sara, you're coming with me.'

'They want you for theft now,' she said, the words tumbling from her mouth in a desperate rush. 'But if you take me with you, they'll add kidnapping to the charge. You'll spend the rest of your life in prison.'

He looked at her, then at the road. Ice gleamed ahead, and he slowed the car.

'The Maharanee of Gadjapur's jewels are worth five million dollars, Sara.' His voice was soft. 'That's grand larceny. I'm a convicted felon. If they catch me, I'll spend at least the next ten years in prison, before I can even hope to get out.'

'Yes, but what's ten years compared to life? A kidnapping charge is——'

'Ten years or life is all the same to me,' he said sharply. 'I'm not going back behind those walls.'

'Why won't you listen to me? I'm trying to help you.'

He turned towards her, and the look he gave her made her shrink back in her seat.

'I'm not a fool, Sara. The only person you're interested in helping is yourself, and the best way you can do that is to shut your mouth. Do you understand?'

Sara nodded. There was a sanded stretch of road

ahead; as soon as the tyres crunched over it, Peter Saxon stepped on the accelerator and the car picked up speed. Sara glanced at the speedometer, watching as the needle passed fifty, touched sixty, and moved beyond it. She thought of what he'd said about staying below the speed limit, but somehow she knew in her heart that no police car would be waiting in the snowbound darkness.

They would travel, unhindered, into the night, and leave Brookville and the only life she had ever known far behind them.

The thought was terrifying. Then why, Sara thought, as she stole a quick glance at the man beside her, why was her heart racing with a kind of wild excitement?

CHAPTER FIVE

'SARA? Are you asleep?'

'Mmm?'

A hand touched her cheek. 'It's time to rise and shine, Sara. Do you hear me?'

Sara's eyes flew open. 'Of course I hear you,' she said, pulling away from his touch. 'I wasn't sleeping.'

He laughed softly. 'My error. I thought you might be—and I hated to wake you. You looked very peaceful, snuggled down inside my coat that way.'

Sara's cheeks reddened. 'I was just resting my eyes,' she said, shoving his coat down to her waist. 'Where are we, anyway?'

'We're coming into a town called Central Falls. It's our last stop.'

Our last stop. Sara sat up straight and stared out of the window. He'd said they were going to the Adirondacks, but this place didn't look very mountainous. They were on a two-lane road, slick with snow and ice. Darkened houses and shop-fronts lined the way.

The dashboard clock read one fifty-five. Hell, it was almost two in the morning! The last time she'd looked, it had been midnight, which meant she had slept for more than an hour. But that was impossible. The few times she had been away from home, she'd lain awake half the night, unable to sleep in a strange bed.

Sara ran her fingers through her loose hair, trying to tame the tangled strands. For a woman who couldn't sleep in a strange bed, she'd certainly had no difficulty sleeping in a strange car, with a strange man beside her.

Exhaustion. That was the reason. Her body and mind were just fatigued by all that had happened to her in the past hours. And she ached all over. Her back, her shoulder, her hip—the fall on the ice in the bank car park, she thought, remembering. She held her breath and flexed her foot gingerly. There was a dull, throbbing pain, but nothing she couldn't handle. The ankle joint moved easily. Would it hold up if she got the chance to make a break for freedom? All she could do was pray it would.

The car was impossibly warm. The heater was still turned way up, and, on top of that, she had been bundled in Peter Saxon's coat. Even now, with the coat in her lap, she could still feel the heat of it surrounding her. It had almost been as if she were in his arms . . .

She shifted uneasily, and looked at him. 'What did you say this town was called?'

'Central Falls. We're in the Adirondack foothills.'

Sara peered out the window. It was still snowing, but the flakes were larger and fell like lazy feathers from the dark sky, blanketing everything with a pristine hush.

Peter Saxon was driving fairly slowly; she wondered if it was the slick road or the police he was worried about. The road, she thought. There was no sign of life in the arctic world outside the car.

'Does this road lead into the mountains?'

He nodded. 'Yes. It's like a roller-coaster from here on.'

No wonder he'd said this was their last stop. Peter Saxon had coaxed his rental car along the icy surfaces and blowing snow of the highway, but there was no way he would ever get it up a snow-covered mountain road. He was heading for the Adirondack Mountains, he had said, and Sara's imagination had conjured up an

isolated mountain cabin, high in the wilderness near the
Canadian border. She sighed with relief. All the time,
he'd been heading for a town—a town that would, by
daylight, be alive with people and cars and . . .

He swung the wheel to the right. The car crossed the
deserted road and the tyres crunched on to the snowy
shoulder, spun uselessly for a few seconds, then gripped
the surface. The car began moving slowly ahead.

Sara stared out of the window, trying to make sense
of their surroundings. Row after row of snow-covered
vehicles lay ahead. They had driven into some kind of
car park.

'What are you——?'

'Keep quiet!'

Peter Saxon's voice, so soft when he had awakened
her moments before, was hard and commanding. He
reached out and turned off the headlights. The night,
and the falling snow, gathered them up as the car moved
slowly through the car park.

Suddenly, a sign loomed ahead. 'Carroll's Clean
Cars,' it read. 'No Money Down.'

Beside her, Peter Saxon chuckled. 'And a damned
good thing that is,' he said softly. 'No money down is
just about as much as we can afford.'

Sara turned towards him. It was hard to see his face
clearly in the faint glow of the dashboard and the pale
illumination of the snow, but she glimpsed dark
smudges of fatigue beneath his eyes, and faint lines
beside his mouth. Still, there was a ring of something in
his voice that might have been excitement.

'What are we doing here?' she asked softly.

He gave her a quick smile. 'We're shopping.'

'Shopping?'

He nodded. 'We need wheels, Sara. This baby's been
good enough until now, but she'll never make it into

the mountains.'

'I thought—you said we'd reached the end of the line——'

'We have, with this car. We need something with four-wheel drive if we're going to get any further. Something tough and——' He drew in his breath. 'Something like that Bronco,' he said, swinging the wheel to the left. 'There we are, Sara. The chariot of my dreams.'

He switched off the ignition. They glided forward silently for a few yards, and then stopped beside a powerful vehicle that looked to be part truck, part car.

'A four-by-four,' Sara said, her voice as low-pitched as Peter Saxon's had been.

He laughed. 'You're full of surprises. What would you know about four-by-fours?'

She shrugged her shoulders. 'The department owns one. Chief Garrett uses it when the roads are bad.'

'Clever man, Chief Garrett.' He released his seat-belt, then looked at her. 'OK,' he whispered, 'let's go.'

Sara stared at him. 'You're not going to steal that Bronco, are you?'

He grinned. 'Semantics, Sara. If it makes you feel any better, think of it as a trade. I'll leave my car in its place.'

He reached for the door-handle, and she put her hand on his arm. 'It's not your car. It's rented.'

He shrugged. 'Semantics again. I'll settle my bill with "Carroll's Clean Cars" another time. But for now——'

'You can't do this,' Sara insisted.

His eyebrows rose. 'Really?'

'This is—it's wrong, Mr Saxon. It's——'

He laughed unpleasantly. 'Have you forgotten what's in the trunk of this car, Sara?'

'Mr Saxon, for heaven's sake, you're just making

things worse! Car theft will add even more years on to your sentence. When they catch you——'

'*If* they catch me. Only *if* they catch me. Now, please, get out of the car.'

'Of course they will. It's just a matter of time.' He said nothing, and she took a deep breath. 'What you should do is give yourself up. The court might be more lenient if you *did. Let me call my boss. He's an understanding man.'

'Yes, I saw just how understanding he was this morning when we met.'

'It was yesterday morning,' Sara said, wondering how that could be true when it felt as if days had gone by instead of hours. 'And you took him by surprise. Let me call him.'

'Get out of the car, Sara.'

'Why won't you listen to reason? Just let me call Chief Garrett.'

Peter Saxon looked at her. 'I'm really touched.' That quick, cynical smile she knew so well spread across his face. 'Such concern for my welfare!'

'Mr Saxon——'

'What ever happened to "Peter"?'

She stared at him. 'What does that have to do with anything?'

He shrugged his shoulders. 'I don't know,' he said, and he smiled at her. 'It just occurred to me that you'd finally started calling me by my first name, and then you stopped again.'

'This is ridiculous. I'm trying to discuss something important, Mr Saxon, and——'

'Peter.'

'Mr Saxon, if you would just listen, I——'

'Peter.' He touched his finger to the tip of her nose. 'I can be as stubborn as you can, Sara. I promise you that.'

She shook free of his hand. 'I don't understand you at all,' she snapped. 'How you can sit here and joke, when half the police in New York State are looking for you?'

'Was it the sight of the jewels in my boot that shocked you into formality, Sara?'

Sara gritted her teeth. 'It was a sight that would have shocked anybody, Mr Saxon. It was——'

'No, come to think of it, you had gone back to calling me "Mr Saxon" even before we ran off the road. You——'

Sara slammed her hand against the dashboard. 'You were damned lucky that was *all* I called you,' she said furiously. 'After the way you played with me in the green——' Her eyes widened as she realised what she'd said. Peter's teasing smile faded, and he caught her hands in his.

'So,' he said softly, 'the truth at long last. Is that what you thought I was doing?'

'It doesn't matter. What counts is——'

'It matters to me.' His fingers wove through hers. 'Was that why you ran away? Because you thought I was playing games?'

'No,' she said. 'I mean, I didn't think anything. And I didn't run away. I told you, I wanted to go home.'

His gaze moved over her face like a caress. 'Did you, now?'

'Yes,' Sara said desperately. 'Mr Saxon——'

'Peter.'

'This is insane! Here I am, trying to make you listen to reason . . .'

He lifted one hand to her face, and lay it against her cheek. 'You're so serious about everything, Sara. So determined.'

'Of course I am,' she said, trying to ignore the feel of his fingers against her skin. 'If you give yourself up, if you let me go . . .'

His eyes darkened. He moved his hand into her hair, letting the silken strands tangle in his fingers.

'Is that what you really want?' His voice was a whisper in the darkness. 'Do you want me to let you go, Sara?'

'Yes,' she said quickly. Too quickly. What's the matter with you, Sara? Why do you sound so breathless? 'Of course I want that. Why wouldn't I? You——'

'Shall I show you the reason, sweet Sara?'

She tried to draw back as he bent towards her, but his hand held her fast. His breath warmed her lips, and then his mouth touched hers. His kiss was gentle, as light as the touch of a snowflake, but it sent waves of sweet warmth shimmering through her body.

'Don't,' she whispered when he lifted his head, but her eyes closed when he moved towards her and kissed her again.

His lips moved gently on hers, as if asking something of her in return. Her hands came up between them and spread on his chest. She wanted to push him from her but, when she felt the heavy beat of his heart beneath her palms, her own heart began to race.

What was happening to her? Her quickening pulse whispered of more than fear. His mouth was on her temple, his lips warm and moist.

'Sara,' he murmured, and his hands clasped her shoulders. 'Sara.'

Don't let him do this to you. He thinks you're a naïve fool, Sara. This is the same way he treated you before, only now the stakes are higher. You're his prisoner, Sara. His prisoner . . .

'Let go of me,' she demanded, wrenching free of his grasp. She drew a deep breath, and forced her eyes to meet his. 'I suppose you think I don't know what's going on.'

His eyes searched hers. 'No,' he said softly, 'I'm not sure you do.'

She wanted to look away from the penetrating brown gaze, but she forced herself not to.

'If there's any decency in you, Mr Saxon, you'll let me go.'

He shook his head. 'I'm sorry, Sara.'

'You don't need me,' she said in a hurried whisper. 'You—you could probably move faster without me. And . . .'

He looked at her, and his eyes grew dark. 'But I do need you, Sara.'

She shook her head. 'You could let me out here, before you go any further. I wouldn't be able to tell them anything. I don't know where you're headed——'

'To Indian Lake Lodge.'

Sara put her hands over her ears. 'I don't want to hear it,' she said. 'I don't want to know anything.'

Peter Saxon caught her by the wrists, and pulled her hands down. 'You know all that matters,' he said with sudden ferocity. 'You know that I have the jewels.'

She looked at him blankly. 'Everyone knows that.'

His mouth twisted. 'Everyone assumes it. But only you can prove it.' His hands tightened on hers. 'I'll never let you go, Sara. Do you understand?'

Her heart began to race like a metronome out of control. 'You don't mean that.'

'Maybe you didn't pay attention to what I said before. I told you I was never going to be locked up again.'

'You should have thought of that before you stole

those jewels.'

A tight smile curved across his mouth. 'This is a charming little chat, but we're going to have to cut it short. You were right—it's crazy to waste all this time.' He let go of her and opened his door. Cold air swept into the car. 'Just remember what I told you earlier. Behave yourself, and you'll come through this all right.'

Her heart thudded. 'Why should I believe that?' she asked. Her eyes met his. 'Because you're a man of honour?'

A sudden tension narrowed his mouth. 'Would you believe me if I said I were?'

The breath hissed from her. 'No. Not unless you let me go——'

'Just don't force my hand, Sara. Do you understand?'

She nodded, and the muscles in her neck felt rigid. 'Yes.'

'Good. Now, get out of the car. I want you where I can keep my eyes on you. And keep down—we're pretty well hidden from the road, but I'm not taking any chances.'

The night was silent and cold as death. Sara stepped from the car and held his coat out to him, but he shook his head.

'It'll only hamper my movements,' he said. 'Put it on—you're shaking already.'

She opened her mouth to tell him she was fine, that she didn't need anything of his. But she was already shivering, and she clamped her lips together.

What was the point in freezing? She would never be able to escape if she turned into a lump of ice. Peter Saxon had watched her like a hawk so far, but he couldn't keep that up indefinitely.

She watched as he opened the boot of the car and

rummaged in the tool-box, where the jewels he'd stolen blazed with fire. But he barely looked at them. Instead, he pulled out a piece of wire and a screwdriver, and within seconds the car was open. Then he walked to the rear of the car and bent down.

What kind of man could steal five million dollars' worth of gems, and then treat them with such cool disinterest? They had been together for hours now, and, the more the time passed, the less she understood Peter Saxon.

He was unscrewing the licence-plate, his hands sure and steady. Sara's glance moved slowly over his face. His eyes were narrowed with concentration; his mouth was drawn into a hard, cold line. But it wasn't hard and cold, she thought crazily. His mouth was warm and exciting, its taste sweet.

He rose to his feet and their eyes met. Sara flushed and turned away. Yes, she thought, yes, she would make her break for freedom soon, and damn the consequences. More than anything, she wanted to be back in her own world, where life was safe.

'Hold this.'

He handed her the closed tool-kit. It felt surprisingly light, considering the fortune it held. Peter Saxon blew on his hands, then knelt beside the front of the car. Seconds later, he had attached the car's plates to the Bronco.

'Any policeman who checks will know those plates are registered to a different vehicle,' Sara said, and then could have bitten her tongue off for having said it.

He looked at her, and smiled unpleasantly. 'I keep forgetting about your police background, Sara. You're right, of course. But the cops will be looking for a late model black Ford, not this. And,' he added, pulling a small folding-knife from his pocket, 'we'll make it just a bit difficult for them.' Quickly, he cut the wires to the light that illuminated the number-plate.

'Remarkable, the things one learns in gaol,' Sara said coolly.

He looked at her and laughed softly. 'Yes, isn't it?' She watched as he used a length of clear plastic tubing to siphon petrol from his car to the new one. Finally, he took the tool-box from her, and tossed it inside the Bronco. 'All right, get in.'

She climbed in stiffly, wincing as she put weight on her injured ankle. But Peter Saxon didn't notice; he slammed the door after her, then hurried around to the driver's side.

'OK,' he murmured as he got in, 'here comes the hard part.' He leaned towards the dashboard, shoulders blocking Sara's view. 'I've never tried this before, but I had a cellmate who swore it was child's play. Chico said all you had to do was . . .' he grunted as the lock snapped and fell away from the steering column '. . . then find the right wires and . . .' His breath hissed between his teeth as the Bronco's engine sputtered, then turned over. 'Another lesson learned, courtesy of the New York State penal system,' he said, and he shifted into gear and looked over at Sara. 'Ready?'

She stared at him. 'Have I a choice?'

Something sprang to life deep in his eyes. 'What if I decided to give you one, sweet Sara? Would you really leave me now?'

Her breathing quickened. 'I . . . I . . . yes,' she said, 'yes, of course.'

Their eyes met and held, and then he laughed. 'Then it's a damned good thing I'm not giving you one,' he said, and he stepped on the accelerator.

The Bronco rolled across the car park and on to the road. At first, Sara waited for the engine to cough and die. But, as the miles rolled away, she began to think 'Carroll's Clean Cars' had put the lie to all the jokes she'd ever heard about used-car dealers. Either that, or Peter Saxon had made a good choice. They were moving swiftly north-west, leaving Central Falls and rescue behind.

Within half an hour, the road was almost impassable. Certainly, the car they had ditched would never have made it through all this snow and ice. It was hard going, even for the Bronco. And, the further they travelled, the more desolate the wilderness outside became.

'Do you know where you're going?' Sara asked finally. 'I haven't seen a light or a house.'

'There's a town just ahead.' Peter Saxon glanced at the dashboard, and then at the road. 'At least, I hope there is. We're almost out of petrol.'

Her gaze followed his. The petrol-gauge needle hovered just near 'empty'.

'What makes you think there's a town?' A shudder ran through her. 'It doesn't look as if anything's out there except forest.'

'There's a town,' he said positively. 'I remember it.'

She looked at him in surprise. 'You mean, you've been here before?'

He nodded. 'Many times. There's not only a town, there's a petrol station and café that stays open all night for the truckers. Thompson took us there a couple of times, when he had to have the car fixed.'

'Us?'

'My brother and me. Thompson let us tag along with him . . .'

Sara looked at him. 'And who was Thompson?'

'Our grandfather's chauffeur. We spent most of one winter traipsing around after him.' He laughed. 'Poor guy. We probably drove him crazy.'

Sara had a sudden vision of a pair of spoiled teenagers tormenting the beleaguered family chauffeur with demands for driving lessons.

'The poor-little-rich-kid syndrome,' she said coldly. 'And so, forlorn and misunderstood, you turned to a life of crime.'

He laughed, but it was a sharp, humourless sound. 'I was seven years old—a long way from what you so graciously called "a life of crime". And I had no idea I was rich. Neither did Johnny—he was only a year older than me. All we knew was that we had suddenly been taken from the only home we'd ever known, and plunked down in a place so alien it might as well have been Mars.'

Sara looked at him curiously. 'Here, you mean? Well, I admit, it's pretty isolated in these mountains. But——'

'We grew up in a place called called Chahulamec, Sara. It's six thousand miles and a thousand years from Indian Lake Lodge.'

'Indian Lake Lodge? That's where we're going, isn't it?'

Peter nodded. 'It belongs to my grandfather.' His teeth gleamed in a quick grin. 'Just listen to me,' he said. 'The old man's been dead four years, and I talk about him as if he were still sitting behind his desk.' Suddenly, he leaned forward and wiped his hand across the windscreen. 'Hey,' he said, 'did you see that?'

Sara stared out the window. 'What?'

'A light. I thought I saw a light ahead. It might be that petrol station.' He sighed, and settled back in the seat. 'It sure as hell better be. If we don't find it soon . . .'

But Sara's thoughts were far from the narrow road and the winter night. 'What did you mean about that town—Chahutamec—being a thousand years from here?'

'It's called Cha*hula*mec,' he said, changing gear as the hill they were climbing became steeper. 'It's in Brazil, on the Amazon River.'

'The Amazon?' she repeated.

He laughed. 'Yeah. Headhunter country.'

Sara stared at him. 'Is that where you were born?'

'No, my parents made sure each of us was born in the good old USA. But they took us to the Amazon when we were babies. It was the only home we'd ever known until they died. And then——'

His tone was so matter of fact that she almost missed what he had said.

'They died? Both your parents?'

He nodded. 'They were lost in an accident on the river. Their dugout was overturned, and . . .'

She wondered, for a moment, if he were making the story up as he went along. But some instinct told her he wasn't. There was a curious flatness in his voice, in his eyes, that told her Peter Saxon was telling her more about himself than he'd intended. He paused, then cleared his throat.

'Keep an eye out for that petrol station, will you? I'd hate to end up running out of petrol on a night like this.'

Sara looked at him. 'That must have been hard for you and your brother—losing your folks when you were so young.'

Peter Saxon nodded again. 'At least we had each other. We were so close then . . .' His words drifted away.

'Aren't you still?' She looked at him curiously. 'Close, I mean. You said——'

'My brother's dead.' His voice was hard and flat. 'And all this is ancient history.'

Something stirred within Sara's breast. She wanted to

reach out and put her hand on his . . .

'I'm sorry,' she said softly.

Peter shrugged his shoulders. 'It doesn't matter. I haven't thought of any of it in years.' He turned to her, and gave her a quick smile. 'Not until today, when I remembered Indian Lake Lodge.'

She smiled back. 'And Thompson.'

Peter laughed, and the almost palpable tension in the car eased. 'And Thompson—who has my everlasting gratitude because there, ye of little faith, is the petrol station I promised!'

Sara smiled back at him. 'There it is, indeed,' she said. 'And it still stays open all night.'

She watched him from beneath her lashes as he drove across the road and pulled to a stop beside a petrol pump. What must it have been like, she wondered, to be seven years old and to lose both your parents? What must it have been like to find yourself taken from the only home you had known, a place of colour and sun, and brought here to this harsh world of cold and wind? And when had he lost his brother? Now that she thought about it, hadn't there been some mention of it in the newspaper accounts of Peter's capture?

Suddenly, something he had said flashed into her mind. She looked at him in the darkness, and she cleared her throat.

'Peter?' He turned to her, and she gave him a hesitant smile. 'What you said about the chauffeur, that you traipsed after him . . . Why was that? I mean, where was your grandfather?'

'I told you, Sara, it's ancient history. It's not important.'

'Maybe it's important to me.'

The words tumbled into the silence. He looked into her eyes, and then he shrugged.

'Grandfather was not partial to small children.' He smiled, but his eyes were empty. 'His phrase, Sara, not mine.'

There was a knock on the door. Both Peter and Sara looked up, startled. The petrol station attendant stood beside the Bronco, eyebrows raised.

'Fill it up?' he mouthed.

Peter nodded. 'Yes.' He opened the door, and stepped out into the cold. 'Check the oil, too. And I need some windscreen washer fluid. And an ice scraper. A good one. And . . .'

His voice faded as he closed the door after him, and followed the attendant to the office. Sara watched them, then drew Peter's coat more closely around her, and settled into her seat to wait for him to return.

It was only when he came back to the Bronco long moments later, and climbed inside, that she realised he'd left her alone. She could have got away easily, she thought. All she'd had to do was open the door and step out.

But she hadn't.

CHAPTER SIX

THEY reached the lodge just before dawn—at least, Peter said they had reached it. Sara could see only the icy ribbon of road stretching ahead. It looked the same as it had for the past endless miles.

'There's the lodge,' he said suddenly.

Sara sat forward and stared out of the window. 'I don't see anything.'

She felt strange—apprehensive and excited all at once, and she wondered if he could hear it in her voice. But all his concentration was on the road, just as it had been ever since they'd left the petrol station, and she thought, not for the first time, that his tension had as much to do with where they were headed as with the icy roads.

'You will, in a few minutes. It's hidden by the trees now, but just as soon as we get to the top of this rise——' An ominous metallic clatter rose from under the Bronco's hood, and Peter drew in his breath. 'Come on,' he whispered, 'don't fail me now, not when we're this close.'

Sara sank back in the seat. The road was relatively clear of snow. The trees on either side of it were tall, and their branches met overhead in a protective canopy. Still, it was a miracle the stolen vehicle had got them as far as it had. It had begun wheezing and groaning just after they left the petrol station. Peter had slammed his hand on the steering wheel in frustration, and alternately coaxed and cursed the Bronco up the dark, winding road.

'Maybe you should turn back,' Sara had suggested, but he'd shaken his head.

'We'll make it.'

One look at his face told her that they would, indeed, make it, if grim determination had anything to do with it. After that, all his energies had been focused on the icy road and the dying Bronco. He had never realised that she'd let her chance to escape slip away.

As the miles and the minutes passed, she brooded about what had happened, playing the scene over in her mind, hoping eventually to find some clue that would explain why she had sat waiting for Peter to return to the car, instead of throwing open the door and racing for freedom.

The station had been brightly lit, as had the café beside it. And there had been trucks parked in front, which meant people inside. And telephones. And . . .

And she hadn't done a thing. Why? No matter how she tried, she couldn't come up with an answer. After a while, she pushed the whole incident to the back of her mind.

There were more urgent things to worry about, she told herself. The strange sounds coming from the Bronco, for example, and the road that had become a glittering strand of ice. And overriding everything was the almost palpable tension of the man beside her.

It seemed as if, the closer they got to the lodge, the more silent he became. By the time he turned off the main road and on to a frozen track that wound through the forest like a dark snake, Sara's nerves were at breaking point.

'It's crazy to try and get up a mountain in weather like this,' she said.

Peter glanced at her, then back at the road. 'There's only a little further to go. We're on Saxon land now.'

'Then where's the lodge? Shouldn't we see it soon?'

He laughed then, although there was no humour in the sound. 'My grandfather owned half this mountain, Sara. He built the house where he could be sure of his privacy.' The Bronco groaned as he shifted. 'When you see the top of the mountain, you'll see the house.'

But there was still no sign of a house, or a cabin, or whatever it was that lay ahead. A few minutes ago, he had said the house was just ahead, at the top of the rise. But they were almost at the top now; the road was, in fact, widening, and . . .

Sara drew in her breath. Ahead, in a clearing, shimmering ghostly grey in the light of the winter dawn, a massive structure of dark stone and darker wood stood brooding, indifferent to man and weather. A frozen lake, pristine and glistening, lay behind it. Beyond, mountains raised their shoulders against the milky sky, their peaks lost in the clouds that warned of yet more snow.

Peter jammed on the brakes, and the Bronco lurched to a stop.

'There it is,' he said softly.

Sara swallowed drily. 'I didn't expect—I thought it would be a summer cottage,' she said. 'A cabin——'

He laughed and shifted into gear. 'Twenty-two rooms and ten baths, Sara. A private lake, a small fleet of boats.' The Bronco rolled forward. 'Welcome to Indian Lake Lodge.'

They drove past the house to the attached garage. It was, Sara thought, almost as large as her house in Brookville. She looked back at the dark forest and shuddered.

'I don't like it here,' she whispered.

Peter brushed her cheek with the tips of his fingers. 'No,' he said softly, 'neither do I. But it's safe. No one knows about this place—it was Grandfather's private refuge from the city, and he never brought anyone up here with him.' His eyes grew clouded. 'I should have sold it after he died.'

Sara looked at him. 'Why didn't you?'

'That's a good question. I don't know—the ghosts, maybe.' He smiled at the expression that came over her face. 'Good ones.'

'I don't understand, Peter. How can——?'

A sudden frigid wind swept across the lake, rattling the Bronco and throwing up a screen of drifting snow. Peter turned up his collar and reached for the door-handle.

'We're wasting time. It's going to take me a couple of minutes to break in——'

'Break in? But you said the place was yours.'

'I didn't plan on ever coming here again, Sara.' He opened the door, then looked at her. 'Can you drive one of these things?' When she nodded, he flashed her a smile. 'OK. Just see that the engine doesn't die.'

He took a screwdriver from the dashboard, then stepped out into the cold morning. Sara slipped behind the steering wheel, watching as he bent over the padlock on the door. The engine coughed, and she tapped her foot gently on the accelerator.

Shift into reverse, Sara. Shift into reverse and leave him here.

'Sara?' She blinked and looked up. The outbuilding door was open, and Peter was waving her forward. She put the Bronco into gear, let it roll forward, and the door fell shut behind her.

He stepped into the cab and reached past her to the wires he had joined together hours before.

'Done,' he said, and pulled the wires apart.

The Bronco's engine shuddered into silence.

The garage was cavernous. The light was poor—it came from the only unboarded window—but there was enough for Sara to see the strange assortment of cars around them. There was a vintage something or other, expensive-looking even with dust lying on it in thick layers. There was a jeep, with the words 'Indian Lake Lodge' discreetly etched in gold leaf on the door. There was even a vehicle that, except for its wide, deeply cleated tyres, was a near-cousin of the Bronco. Peter patted it fondly as he walked past it.

'There you are, baby,' he said, and he smiled at Sara. 'Our ticket out.'

She wanted to ask him what that was supposed to mean, but he was already standing beside a padlocked door she assumed connected the garage to the house, a look of rapt concentration on his face. His fingers danced across the lock and the door swung open.

'Welcome to Indian Lake Lodge, *madame*,' Peter said, giving her a deep, mocking bow. 'All the comforts of the finest hotels—and the charm of the most expensive mausoleums. Would you like the grand tour now, or after I've shown you to your accommodation?'

Sara ran her tongue over her lips. 'What's that sound?'

He cocked his head and listened for a few seconds. 'Sounds like the demons of hell, doesn't it?' He smiled and held out his hand. 'It's only the wind cutting across the lake. Come on, Sara. It's not as bad as it looks.'

She stepped down from the Bronco. It was the first time she'd put any weight on her ankle in hours, and the sudden pressure was painful. She cried out and grabbed for the car door, but before she reached it Peter was beside her. His arms closed tightly around her.

'Sara? What is it?'

'My ankle.' Her breath hissed between her teeth.

'I sprained it when I fell in the bank car park.'

He swung her into his arms, and strode through the open door and into the house.

'Why the hell didn't you tell me?' he demanded, kicking the door closed behind him. 'For all you know, it's broken.'

Sara shook her head. 'It isn't,' she said, 'it's just a sprain. Please, Peter, put me down.'

His only answer was to draw her more closely against him, as he carried her through the house. The rooms were enormous, filled with massive pieces of sheet-draped furniture. Shutters closed out most of the light, the artificial darkness adding to the gloom. The walls were hung with unsmiling portraits of what Sara assumed were Saxon ancestors. It was hard to imagine a child spending his summers in a house like this, she thought, as Peter shouldered open a door at the far end of the downstairs hall.

This room was smaller than the others, although it still seemed the size of a tennis court. There was a stone fireplace at one end, logs still neatly stacked beside it, a couch drawn up before it. Peter set her down gently on her feet, holding her in the curve of one arm, while he whisked the dust-cover from the couch. Then he lifted her again and lay her down on it.

'Now,' he said briskly, 'let's see that ankle.'

'It's fine. Really. I——'

But he was already squatting at her feet, his hands gentle as he eased off her ruined shoes.

'Your feet are like ice, Sara.'

He rubbed them gently, then drew her tattered skirt to mid-calf. 'Dammit, Sara, your ankle's swollen.'

'Please, Peter, it'll be all right. I——'

His hand closed lightly around her foot and he tilted it up. 'Does that hurt?' She shook her head. 'That?'

'A little. But——'

'Move your foot, Sara. Does it hurt there? OK, now from side to side.'

He knelt beside her, moving her foot through a simple series of motions, his touch firm yet gentle. Sara watched his bent head. His hair was dark and thick and a little too long; it curled lightly against the nape of his neck and behind his ears. He needed a haircut, she thought absently, and her hand lifted slowly towards him.

What would happen if she put her palm against the back of his neck? Would his hair feel soft and alive beneath her fingers? She remembered the feel of his moustache against her mouth. Would it feel that way to touch her lips to his neck?

Oh, hell!

Sara snatched back her hand and buried it in her lap, praying Peter couldn't hear the sudden loud hammering of her heart.

'It doesn't seem broken,' he said finally. 'Let me find something to strap it with, and——'

'It doesn't need strapping,' she said, pulling her foot from his hands and swinging it to the floor. 'Really, I'm all right.'

He rose slowly to his feet and looked down at her. 'Yes,' he said softly, 'you are.'

Their eyes met and held, and then Sara wrenched her gaze away. 'You—you promised me a tour of this place, didn't you?'

It seemed a long time before he nodded. 'That's right, I did.' He smiled at her. 'But that was before I realised it was almost as cold in the house as it is outside.' He rubbed his hands together, then bent to the fireplace. 'Let me build a fire to take the chill off the room, Sara. Then I'll find us some warm clothing and take you on a guided tour of the Saxon mausoleum, with a first stop in the kitchen. You must be starved.'

Her stomach growled softly in response, and she laughed. 'I am, indeed.' She watched as he began to lay the fire. 'That's a terrible thing to call a house, you know.'

'A mausoleum?' He shrugged his shoulders. 'Yeah, I suppose it is. But it's appropriate.' He bent and blew softly on the kindling he had lit. 'There was never any life in this place. Cook told me it had always been that way, even when my father was growing up.'

'Cook?'

'She was my other ally. She used to hide chocolate cookies behind the oatmeal boxes in the pantry, so I could have some with my bedtime cocoa.' He grinned. 'Johnny preferred vanilla wafers. Grandfather didn't approve, of course.'

'Your grandfather must have been a hard man,' Sara said slowly.

'He was like steel. Unbending, unyielding, cold——'

'Was your father like that?'

Peter smiled. 'No, he was nothing like that. I can remember him riding me on his shoulders in the rain forest, so I could see the wild orchids and the blue butterflies.'

'And your mother?' Sara prompted gently. 'What was she like?'

He looked at her. 'She was tall, with smiling eyes and a quick laugh.' His face grew clouded. 'It was so long ago, Sara. I wish to hell I could remember them more clearly.'

'It must have been terrible to lose them both. You were so young . . .'

Peter nodded. 'It was hell,' he said quietly. 'For a long time after they died, I hated them.'

'Oh, Peter.' Her voice was low and filled with compassion. 'I'm sure that's not unusual. You were just a child—you probably felt abandoned. You didn't understand death.'

His head lifted sharply, and she saw a terrible coldness in his face. 'Maybe. But part of it was my grandfather's doing. He told me things——'

Sara stared at him. 'I don't—I don't understand.'

He put his foot on the raised hearth, bent his head and stared into the flames.

'I was here, in this house, when they died, Sara. You see, my grandfather had fallen ill, and my parents flew back to see him. My father was still trying to mend old quarrels, I guess, and we came here to spend a few days with him. I don't remember much about the visit—except that I hated this house. I couldn't wait to go back to Brazil . . .'

His words trailed away. Sara waited for him to begin again. Finally, she put her hand lightly on his shoulder.

'What happened?'

Peter shrugged. 'I don't know all the details. Something came up—some deadline that had to be met if my father's grant was to be renewed. My parents had to fly back, but I had a cold or the flu or some damned thing.' He drew in his breath slowly, then let it out. 'My grandfather convinced them to take Johnny and go on without me. He said he would send me along when I was better.'

'And?' Sara asked in a whisper. She could see a knot of muscle move in his jaw. His hands spread on the mantel, the fingers white with tension.

'And they died,' he said in a flat voice. 'My grandfather called me into his office one morning. I can still see him, sitting behind his big desk, his eyes cold behind his wire-rimmed glasses. ''I have unpleasant news for you, boy,'' he said. And then he told me they were dead.'

'Just like—just like that?'

He turned towards her. 'Exactly like that. I remember I started to cry, and he told me to stop, that men didn't behave like sissies. And then he said he had work to do, that I should go to my room and read my Bible, and later he and I would talk about how I could best live my life.'

'But you were just a little boy, Peter! How could he——?'

'When he sent for me again, he told me it was important I understand that my parents' deaths were their own fault. He said he would tell the same thing to Johnny, just as soon as he arrived. My father had no business being in a place like the rain forest, he said. He told me my father had always been selfish and irresponsible, but he would see to it my brother and I grew up to be different.'

Sara looked at him in horrified disbelief. 'How cruel,' she whispered. 'You must have been heartbroken. You must have felt abandoned and deserted and . . .'

He nodded again, his eyes dark with memory. 'All of that and more. I grew up hating my parents for their deaths—and yet, each time the old man talked about them, each time he said I was turning out just like my father, I felt this strange kind of—of joy.'

'And your brother? Did he feel the same way?'

Peter's mouth twisted. 'Yes, I think so. I remember the way we used to look at each other whenever Grandfather accused us of being just like our father . . .'

He fell silent. Sara put her hand on his arm. 'Why did he do it, Peter?'

Peter shrugged his shoulders. 'I suppose he was trying to make certain we would despise our father so much,

we wouldn't want to be like him. You see, our father
had been a great disappointment to Grandfather. He
was an adventurer, not a businessman. He refused to
follow the old man into the Saxon business empire; he
wanted to study cultural anthropology instead.'

'And your grandfather wouldn't let him?'

'That's right. So he worked his way through college.
That was when he met my mother—she was a painter.
They married, and my father got a small grant to study
in Brazil.' He drew a deep breath. 'Grandfather never
forgave him.'

'How did you finally learn the truth? Did your
grandfather tell you?'

'He never told me a damned thing, Sara. By the time I
was in my teens, I had turned myself inside out, trying
to please him, trying not to be what he said I was—a
duplicate of my ne'er-do-well father—and it was hell. I
was like two people: one who wanted to climb
mountains and do something exciting with my life, and
one who felt obligated to make up for my father's sins.
It was the same for my brother.'

Sara was almost afraid to breathe. The crystal
moment seemed too fragile. She felt as if she were being
handed a piece of a jigsaw puzzle that would only fit
into a dimly perceived picture.

'What happened?' she asked finally, her voice barely
a whisper.

'We read our father's journals. It was Johnny's
twenty-first birthday—the journals were his inheritance.
I remember he stayed locked in his room with them all
day, and then, that night, he handed them to me and he
said, ''Welcome to manhood, little brother.''' He drew
a deep breath. 'It was all there—the quarrels, the
bitterness, the attempts to force my father into line.
And then came the entries about my mother, how much

in love they were, and then my brother's birth and mine, and their joy in having us.' He paused, then went on, 'The journals—the last few—were filled with the spirit of life, Sara, the spirit of my father and my mother.'

Peter reached for her hand and clasped it tightly. The room filled with silence.

'Peter?' He looked at her, and she cleared her throat. 'What—what happened to your brother? I seem to remember something about an accident a few years ago——'

Pain lanced across his face. 'Yes. He had gone sky-diving. He'd been jumping for years, but this time—this time his chute didn't open. Grandfather said it was—he said it only proved Johnny was as selfish and irresponsible as my father. He said——' The pressure of his hand on hers increased, and then Peter laughed self-consciously. 'You are some piece of work, Sara Mitchell. A certified, qualified, absolutely bona fide shrink spent sixteen months trying to dredge the story of my life out of me when I was in prison, and he didn't get past my date of birth.'

'I'm so sorry, Peter. I wish there were something I could do.'

'You have done something.' He looked deep into her eyes. 'I've never wanted to tell any of that to anyone, Sara. I never even wanted to think about it, even though I know I have to if I'm ever going to get on with my life.'

Sara shook her head. 'I—I don't think I understand, Peter.'

He smiled at her. 'Never mind,' he said softly. 'I only wish—I wish we'd met some other way. I wish I'd walked into that little police station with a traffic ticket in my hand, instead of an invitation to the Winstead party.'

Sara's heart seemed to stand still. She wanted to tell him it didn't matter how they had met. What mattered was that fate had smiled on them and brought them together, that he had changed her life in less than a day, that she had never felt so happy and complete.

But how could she say any of those things to him? None of them made sense. He was running from the law, and she was his captive. That was reality, that was what she had to remember, that was . . .

A burning ember sprang from the fire, and landed with a hiss on the carpet at their feet. Sara jumped back as Peter picked it up, juggled it from hand to hand, and tossed it on to the hearth. When they looked at each other again, the moment of magic had ended.

'Damn!' he said, and then he laughed. 'Well, burning down the mausoleum is one way to warm it.'

Sara smiled. 'A little extreme, though, don't you think?'

He grinned. 'Absolutely. Especially when there's an easier way to solve our problem.' He cocked his head to the side and looked at her. 'What size do you wear, Sara? A ten? An eight?'

She looked at him as if he were crazy. 'Why?'

'Never mind. The only size I'm probably going to come up with is "too large".' He tapped the tip of her nose with his finger. 'Give me five minutes, Miss Mitchell, and I'll bring you some warm clothes. Not the height of fashion, maybe, but warm.'

'Warm is what matters,' Sara said lightly.

Peter laughed. 'Just remember that when you see what I turn up.'

What he turned up was a motley assortment of woollens and corduroys that he dumped on the couch beside her.

'There you go,' he said. 'Take your pick.'

Sara plucked a plaid wool shirt, a navy sweater, navy cords and two pairs of heavy wool socks from the pile.

'The most beautiful stuff I've ever seen,' she declared, and she got to her feet and took a limping step towards the door.

'Where are you going?'

'To change. I——'

The words caught in her throat. Peter had already tossed aside his jacket and tie. He shook his head as he unbuttoned his frilled shirt and pulled it out of his trousers. Firelight laid a golden sheen on his muscled chest and the dark hair that curled over it.

'You'll freeze,' he said matter-of-factly. He kicked off one shoe, then another, reached to the top button of his trousers, and smiled coyly. 'I won't peek if you won't.'

Sara looked into his eyes and saw the repressed laughter in them. Something wild and exciting leaped within her blood, and she nodded.

'It's a deal,' she said.

She thought she saw surprise register in his eyes, before she turned away and began undressing. Her hands shook as she took off her coat and tossed it aside. She undid the buttons that ran the length of her dress and hesitated. He wasn't watching—she was certain of that. Whatever else he might be, he was a man of his word.

'I won't peek if you won't,' he had said.

Still, his very presence was . . . it was . . .

'Ready?'

'No!' Her hands flew as she peeled away the rest of her clothes. She had one quick moment of panic when she realised she had no bra to put on—she'd worn a long slip beneath the dress with a bra built in—and then she tossed her head. She'd always wanted to see how it felt

not to wear one, but her courage had always failed her.
Well, she thought, pulling on the clothing Peter had
brought her, now was the time.

'Ready,' she called, and she turned to face him.

She had expected almost anything: his laughter,
perhaps, when he saw how the clothing hung on her
slender frame, some teasing remark about her
fashionable outfit.

But she hadn't expected the sudden darkening of his
eyes, or the way his breath caught at the sight of her.
She hadn't expected him to look so handsome, either.
Somehow, she had assumed the clothing he'd found
wouldn't fit him any better than it fitted her.

But it did. Peter was wearing a white, cable-knit,
turtleneck sweater that clung to his broad shoulders and
muscled chest, and a pair of faded corduroys that fitted
his lean hips and long legs closely. He looked . . . he
looked . . .

'Beautiful,' he said softly, and she wondered how it
was that he had read her mind—until she realised he was
talking about her.

'Don't be silly,' she said with a nervous smile. 'I'm
not——'

'How come women look so damned sexy in men's
clothes?'

Sara blushed. 'I look messy,' she said, running her
fingers through her hair. 'I need a comb. And a
barrette.'

'Leave your hair loose,' Peter said quickly. He
walked towards her, his eyes riveted on hers. 'You're a
beautiful woman, Sara Mitchell. Why not let the world
see it?'

'I'm not,' she said, and then she cleared her throat.
'Don't—don't look at me that way, Peter. It
embarrasses me.'

He reached out and cupped her face in his hands. 'That's the last thing I want to do to you.' His gaze dropped to her mouth, the heat of it like a kiss, and then he raised his eyes to hers. 'Welcome to my house, Sara,' he said, 'and thank you.'

It was hard to speak. 'For what?' Sara whispered.

Peter's smile made her heart soar. 'For making this mausoleum finally feel like home.'

CHAPTER SEVEN

THE GLOW of the fire danced on the shadowed walls as Sara placed a sterling silver soupspoon into an oyster-white Limoges china bowl, touched a creamy Irish linen table-napkin to her mouth, and smiled at Peter sitting cross-legged beside her on the parquet floor.

'That,' she said, 'was the strangest breakfast I've ever eaten.' A smile curved across her mouth. 'And the best.'

Laughter gleamed in his brown eyes. 'You mean to say this is the first time you've had consommé with sherry, pâté de fois gras, and smoked turkey at eight in the morning?'

She smiled. 'If it had been *my* pantry we'd raided for breakfast, we'd have had to settle for oatmeal and jam.'

Peter grinned as he collected their dishes. 'Remind me to thank Cook for having left such a motley assortment of tinned foods behind.' He rose and pulled on a heavy wool shirt. 'And now, *madame,* I think some coffee would do nicely, don't you agree?'

Sara nodded. 'I'll make it,' she said. 'You did all this . . .'

'And hard work it was, opening all those cans.' He smiled as he buttoned the shirt and put on leather gloves. 'You stay put, Sara. I'm going to have to go out and get a bucket of snow for the coffee. There's no sense in both of us freezing.' He picked up their dishes and looked down at her. 'How's that ankle?'

'Much better.'

'Good.' He started towards the door, and then turned to look at her. 'Coffee doesn't keep you awake, does it?'

Sara looked at him. 'Why?'

'I want to be on the road by late afternoon. We only have time to nap for a few hours.' A quick smile curved over his mouth, barely visible beneath his moustache. 'I wouldn't want to keep you from getting your rest,' he said, as their eyes met.

She felt a blush rise to her cheeks, but the door closed after him before she could come up with an answer. And the teasing glint in his eyes had invited one—she knew that, even though she had no idea how to frame it.

She thought suddenly of the beautiful women who had flung themselves at him at the Winstead party. One of them would have been quick to reply to that kind of remark. But flirting was an art for which she had no talent at all.

Not that she wanted to flirt with Peter Saxon. There had been a subtle change, yes. She wasn't really afraid he would hurt her, but that didn't mean she'd lost her fear.

Now, her fear was not so much about what *could* happen to her, but about what had *already* happened to her. It was a very private, very dark fear. She had yet to put a name to it but, somewhere along the way, Peter Saxon had stopped being the enemy.

And that, of course, made no sense at all.

Sara rose quickly to her feet and jammed her hands deep into her trouser pockets. He hadn't even existed in her life less than a day ago. Now, she felt as if she'd known him forever. Last night, she'd known he was a hard and dangerous felon. Today, she knew he was a man. A handsome man. A passionate one. A man who made her senses come alive in a way they never had before.

He was also a man who had kidnapped her. And he

didn't trust her any more than she trusted him.

'The line is disconnected,' he had said softly, almost conversationally, when he saw her glance at the telephone. 'And we're more than ten miles from the nearest house.'

She'd nodded, as if he were simply telling her about the lodge, but she knew the truth was darker than that. What he'd been doing was reminding her that there was no way out, that no matter what had happened in those few moments after he had told her about his childhood their situation hadn't changed.

He was running from the law. And she was his prisoner.

Sara sank down on the couch again, and lay her head back. She remembered a magic act she had seen when she was a child. The magician hadn't been very good—even she had been able to see the cards he palmed, and the bits of silk streaming from under his cuffs.

But, as his last trick, he'd done something that had left his audience gasping in awe. There had been a rabbit sitting on the table during the performance, a pink-nosed bunny in a wire cage. The magician had taken the rabbit out of its cage, and held it in his hand, high up over the audience.

'Presto chango,' he had said. He'd passed a gossamer silk over the hand that held the rabbit, and suddenly the rabbit had become a dove that flew high into the air.

Wide-eyed, Sara had turned to her mother. 'That was real magic,' she'd whispered.

Her mother had smiled with all the wisdom of adulthood. 'Illusion, dear. That's all it was. There's no such thing as magic.'

Sara sat forward, propped her elbows on her knees, and put her chin in her hands. She was old enough now to know that her mother had spoken the truth.

There was no such thing as magic, there was only illusion. It was illusion that dazzled the mind and awed the spirit.

Which was the real Peter Saxon, and which was illusion? Was he the hard, cold-eyed man who had threatened her with violence? Or was he the man who had held her in his arms and brought a spiralling heat to her blood?

He hated his grandfather, even in death. Yet he was concerned about her cat.

'Hell, Sara, I forgot about that fur-ball of yours. What's going to become of him?' he had said suddenly, as they ate their meal.

She had stared at him blankly. 'What?'

Peter had lowered his soupspoon to the bowl. 'Your cat,' he had said slowly. 'I'd hate to think of him starving—even though he deserves it, considering what he did to my trousers.'

Sara had assured him that Taj had lots of dry food and water on hand, that Alice Garrett had a key to the house and loved cats herself, and all the while she had been staring at Peter, wondering what kind of man thought nothing of theft and abduction, but worried about an animal's welfare.

Illusion and reality. A good magician could blend the two and create magic. He could make his audience see things that didn't exist, and believe things that weren't true.

The door opened, then slammed shut. Cold air swept into the room.

'It's cold as hell out there!' Peter walked to the fireplace and set a cast-iron pot filled with snow carefully on the grate. 'At least it hasn't started snowing again.' He pulled off his gloves and his outer shirt, then rubbed his hands together. 'Coffee coming up, Sara. I couldn't find any sugar, and of course there's no milk, but——'

'I want to know what happens next, Peter.'

He straightened and turned towards her. He looked, she thought, as surprised by what she had said as she was to have said it. The words had tumbled from her mouth without any plan. But that was just as well—if she'd thought it through, her courage might have failed her.

'I told you what happens,' he said finally. 'We have a cup of coffee, we catch some sleep, and then we leave.'

'You know that's not what I meant.'

His eyes narrowed. 'What did you mean, then?'

Sara met his gaze. 'What happens to me? Will you let me go?'

The expression on his face hardened. 'I can't do that, Sara. I've explained that to you.'

'Peter, listen to me. You can't keep running away. Sooner or later——'

He flung his hand up as if to silence her. 'Forget the speeches,' he growled. 'I'm not interested.'

Sara took a step forward. He was angry—she could see it in his eyes and hear it in his voice. But so was she, she thought suddenly. He had no right to toy with her, to alternately frighten her and entice her.

Illusion and reality. Of course. She was Peter's audience; he had been dazzling her with sleight of hand. How much easier it would be for him if she were his willing companion, not his hostage. And if she fell into his arms—into his bed—he could make her do anything he wanted. He could control her completely.

She was so dumb! She'd known the kind of man he was. When had she forgotten? When had she stumbled into his trap and fallen for his lies and his kisses and . . .?

'Let me go,' she whispered, 'or, when they finally catch you, I'll build the cell they lock you in with my own two hands.'

'Damn you to hell, Sara Mitchell!'

He moved towards her quickly, kicking aside the cushions on which they had sat before the fire, his eyes blazing with rage.

'Don't you touch me,' she gasped, but he reached out and caught hold of her shoulders, his fingers pressing into her flesh with such determination that she felt each one mark her with his anger.

'Didn't anybody ever tell you not to play dangerous games, little girl?' He stared down at her, his chin jutting forward, his eyes as dark as the storm clouds that threatened outside.

'Me? Me, playing games?' She made a sound that was half laugh and half sob. 'You're a fine one to talk! You——'

'All that sweet solicitude a while ago.' She stared at him blankly, and his mouth turned down in a grim line. 'I underestimated you, Sara. It never occurred to me that you were setting me up.'

She shook her head. 'What are you talking about? *I* set you up? I——'

His eyes swept over her face with cold contempt. 'Did you really think I'd let you go, just because you patted my head and said a few kind words?'

Was he crazy? He was looking at her as if she—*she*—were the magician, as if she . . .

His hands spread on her shoulders, and he pulled her towards him with a roughness that made her stumble.

'Or was it just for kicks, Sara?' His voice thickened. 'Was it fun, playing with fire?'

A new kind of terror raced through her. 'You let

go of me,' she breathed, banging her fist against his chest. 'Damn you, Peter Saxon——'

His eyes darkened until they were almost black. 'Come on,' he whispered, pulling her against his hard body. 'Come on, Sara. Touch the flame, and see if it'll burn your fingers.' She cried out as his hands tightened, and he lifted her to her toes. 'Touch the flame, Sara,' he said, and his lips came down on hers.

She whimpered against his mouth, crying out as his teeth closed sharply on her lower lip. Her lips parted in pain, and instantly his tongue thrust between them. The heat of his kiss was like fire, searing her flesh.

Sara struggled against him, but his arms held her fast. It was impossible to escape the hard heat of his body, and panic grew within her, spreading dark wings in her chest. She dragged her mouth from his, and drew a shuddering breath.

'Please,' she whispered, 'please——'

'Sara,' Peter said thickly, 'sweet Sara.'

Suddenly his kiss changed, softened, until it was all warm, honeyed sweetness, until he was giving as well as taking.

Sara's fists opened. Her fingers clutched at his sweater, bunching the heavy wool in her hands, and she pressed herself against him, trembling with a need so intense that it was almost pain. He whispered her name against her mouth, and she sagged against him. All the fight and anger ebbed from her body, as a languor unlike any she had ever known threatened to melt her bones.

'Sara.' His hands moved in her hair, cupping her head, tilting her face to his. 'Sara . . .'

There was something in the way he whispered her name that filled her with an ineffable sorrow. Tears rose in her eyes and trembled on her lashes.

'If only you hadn't stolen the Winstead jewels,' she said brokenly. Her hands spread on his chest, and she stared at him. His hands fell to his sides, and she took a step back. 'I—I just don't understand it, Peter.'

'Sara . . .'

She spun away from him, her arms outstretched in a gesture which embraced the entire room—the dusty Waterford chandelier, the Lalique figures on the mantel, the Aubusson rug that stretched pale across the floor.

'Why steal, Peter? Why would a man with all this become a thief? How much money can one man want?'

He looked at her incredulously. 'Money had nothing to do with it.'

Her eyebrows rose. 'What, then? Why would someone break into people's homes in the middle of the night and risk everything, if not for the money? You stole hundreds of thousands of dollars' worth of jewels——'

He shook his head. 'They were all selective sorties, Sara, and not half as profitable as you might think.'

Sara rolled her eyes to the ceiling. 'How admirable! A fussy thief. What do you think you are, for heaven's sake? A modern Robin Hood?'

His smile hardened. 'I don't suppose I can expect you to understand.'

She laughed without humour. 'No, I don't suppose you can. There's no excuse for theft, no matter how the papers romanticise it.'

He moved towards her, silently and swiftly, and caught her by the wrists.

'Do you know what it's like to get in and out of places that are supposed to be impregnable?'

The dark intensity in his eyes frightened her. It took all her strength to hold his gaze.

'You—you almost sound as if you're proud of what you've done. You're a thief, Peter Saxon. You——'

'Offices. Foreign embassies.' Her face paled and he laughed coldly. 'Yes, that's right. And all that I took from them was the knowledge that I'd been able to gain entry.'

Sara stared at him. 'But why?' she whispered. 'Why would anyone take such chances? The risk must be incredible.'

His eyes lit with fire. 'The risk was the reason, Sara.' He shook his head as if to clear it. 'How can I explain it to you? It's—it's as if . . . Have you ever stood on a precipice and looked out over the valley below?'

'No. I mean, yes. Once.' Sara swallowed, her eyes still on his face. 'Once, when I was a little girl. I'd walked up Stone Mountain, and I—I stood on this big rock that jutted out over the town, and I looked down. And—and . . .'

Peter looked into her eyes. 'How did it feel, Sara?' She didn't answer, and he smiled. 'Didn't it feel as if you could almost flap your arms and soar over that valley? Wasn't there a moment when you thought, hell, I can step out into space, I can fly like an eagle?'

She closed her eyes, remembering. 'Yes,' she whispered, and then her lashes lifted and she looked at him. 'But I didn't do it. I knew the reality was that I would plummet to the earth if I tried to fly.'

'Ah, Sara.' His breath warmed her face. 'Trying to fly is what life's all about, don't you see? Otherwise, we're just travellers on the road, moving from start to finish without opening ourselves to the adventure of the journey.'

Sara stared into his face. 'Are you saying—are you saying that's why you steal? Because—because it's exciting?'

He looked at her for a long moment. She thought, at first, that he wasn't going to answer. Then, suddenly, he took a deep breath and let go of her. Away from his embrace, she felt suddenly cold, and she wrapped her arms around herself.

'My brother and I were eleven and twelve when my grandfather sent us to boarding-school.' A bitter smile touched his lips. 'He was disappointed in us, he said. We were showing the same kind of wild traits as our father. So he sent us to a place where they—well, let's just say that the Mangus Military Academy didn't encourage anybody's spirit of adventure. Johnny graduated when he was seventeen, and Grandfather enrolled him at his Alma Mater. I followed a year later.'

Sara's lips parted. What had this to do with what she had asked? she thought, and suddenly she sensed that it had everything to do with it. She sank down on the edge of the couch, watching as Peter bent to the fire and stared into the flames.

'His university was like his house—bleak, lifeless, untouched by the sun. He wanted Johnny to study accounting, and me law. Neither of us wanted to—hell, I didn't want to study at all; I wanted to climb mountains and touch the clouds and . . .' He straightened and brushed his hands on his trousers. 'I despised myself for it. This time, when the old man said, "You're just like your father," I felt as if I'd been convicted of a crime. So I dug in my heels, and studied corporate law. I was to join him in business.'

'And did you? Study corporate law, I mean?'

Peter nodded. 'I enrolled in pre-law courses. I read my way through every damned book in the law library.' He drew a deep breath, then blew it out. 'By my sophomore year, I thought I was going to explode. I hated school, I hated the old man—hell, I hated myself most of all.'

'But you hadn't—you hadn't done anything wrong.'

He laughed. 'You're anticipating my story, Sara. No, that didn't happen until the start of my junior year.' His eyes grew dark with memory, and he turned his back to her and leaned his forearms on the mantel. 'I discovered my singular talent by accident, when I broke into a room in the dormitory next to mine.'

His words hung in the silent room. Sara stared at him, then rose to her feet.

'You broke into——'

Peter nodded. 'It began as a prank. I don't even remember what led up to it, exactly. My brother and I shared a suite with two other guys, and we'd been having trouble with some seniors in the next dormitory. Things got out of hand—they trashed my room-mate's car, that kind of thing.' He smiled. 'And then, one night—after a dozen beers too many—we decided we'd had enough. So we dressed in black, rubbed charcoal on our faces, and dropped a rope from the roof of their building.' His smile twisted. 'It was a six-storey building, Sara, and they lived on the fourth floor.'

'And?' she said softly. 'What happened?'

He turned towards her, his eyes dark. 'The two other guys sobered up fast, just as soon as they saw how black it was on that roof, and how the rope seemed to vanish into space.'

Sara could see him, in her mind's eye. She could almost feel what he had felt, the sudden excitement, the challenge . . .

'But not you,' she said in a whisper.

Peter smiled. 'No, Sara, not me. And not Johnny. The rope looked like—like it led to all the dreams I'd ever had. I hardly breathed as I went down it and into that darkened suite. The plan had been to light some

firecrackers and run like hell, or some such nonsense.'
He took a step towards her. 'But that would have
spoiled it for me. As I stood there, I knew all I wanted
was to carry away the secret knowledge that I'd risked
my neck and done the impossible.'

Sara watched his face. 'So you didn't light the fire-
cracker. You stole something instead, a kind of—a
souvenir——'

Peter's eyes darkened. 'I told you,' he said sharply, 'it
was enough just to know I'd done it.' He looked away
from her. 'Johnny was the one who needed something
more. He took a pencil, or a pack of cigarettes, or some
damned thing to prove he'd been there——'

His words faded away. Sara waited, then cleared her
throat. 'And?' she prompted softly.

It was as if he hadn't heard her. He was in some far-
away place, she could see it in his face. Finally, just as
she was about to speak again, he sighed.

'I suppose it sounds crazy. Hell, it *was* crazy. I knew
that, even then. But I felt so alive; I'd never felt that
way before——'

'And that's why—that's why you steal?'

'I didn't steal.' His voice was harsh. 'I told you
that——'

'You said you didn't take anything that first time, no.
But you did, after that. It's why you went to prison.'

His eyes went flat. 'Prison.' The single word was
filled with malice. 'I thought I'd die in there,' he
whispered. He clasped her shoulders. 'To be caged, like
an animal . . .'

A shudder rippled through him; Sara felt it in her
bones. Her eyes swept his face. It all made a terrible
kind of sense, she thought. What he was describing was
life lived on the edge. How many times had Jim Garrett
said that the best cops could as easily have been on

the other side of the law?

In another century, Peter Saxon would have been a pirate or a mercenary, lauded or hated, depending on which side claimed him.

'I thought I'd die in there. To be caged, like an animal . . .'

Yes, she thought, yes, bars and locks would be a living death to someone like him. Then why . . .? Why . . . ?

'Peter.' Sara touched her tongue to her lips. 'If you'd decided to give it all up—if that's true . . .' She raised her eyes to his. 'If it is, then why did you steal the Winstead jewels?' Her voice grew husky, then broke. 'Dammit, Peter, they'll put you away forever this time. Didn't you think of that?'

In the eerie silence, Sara could hear the wind moaning across the frozen lake. Peter smiled, almost tenderly, and drew her towards him.

'Sara.' His voice was like the whisper of the wind. 'Sweet Sara.'

He caught her face between his hands, and bent his head to her. Sara began to tremble. She had asked him a question to which he had no answer, she thought, but as his lips touched hers neither the question nor the answer mattered. Her lashes fell to her cheeks; slowly, she lifted one arm and curved it around his neck, her fingers tangling in his hair. He whispered her name again, and her mouth opened to his.

Time stood still while their breaths mingled, while she tasted the sweetness of his kiss. It was Peter who finally, gently, put her from him.

'Sara,' he said softly, 'look at me.' Her eyes opened slowly and focused on his. 'I didn't steal the Winstead jewels.'

She felt the heat of her anger as it swept through

her. 'What kind of fool do you take me for, Peter? I saw the jewels, remember? I saw them with my own eyes.'

His hands kneaded her shoulders. 'Listen to me, Sara. I didn't steal them. Someone set me up.'

She was almost afraid to breathe as she searched for the truth in his eyes.

'Whoever did it,' he said, 'expected the theft to be discovered on Monday morning, at the museum. Everything went wrong—I wasn't supposed to look in the tool-box. Something must have happened at the Winstead house, something that set the alarms off.'

'But—but that doesn't make any sense, Peter. If that was true, all you had to do was tell the police you didn't know how the jewels got into your car. You——'

He laughed. 'Think of what you're saying, Sara. The police would never have believed me. Hell, *you* don't believe me.'

'Peter——'

'I'm telling you the truth, Sara.' His fingers bit into her flesh. 'I didn't take the jewels. I was set up.'

She reached up and clasped his hands in hers. 'I don't understand. Who would do such a thing? And why, Peter? Why?'

'I wish to hell I had the answers. Maybe I can get them, given time. But for now, all I can do is get out of the country.'

'Out of——'

'Yes. I'm heading for Canada. I know some people in Montreal—they'll help me.'

'Peter.' She felt breathless, as if she had just run a race. 'Listen to me. If you're innocent——'

'They've set me up too well, don't you see? The only thing I have to go back to is a cell.' His voice dropped to a whisper. 'Who would believe my story?'

Was he telling her the truth? She wanted to believe him. Oh, how she wanted to believe him.

'Go back,' she said. 'I'll tell them——'

'Tell them what? That you saw the jewels in the boot?' She said nothing, and he moved closer to her. 'Do you believe me, Sara?'

Sara hesitated. 'I—I don't know. I——'

He bent to her and kissed her again—a slow, deep kiss that set her pulse rocketing.

Don't be stupid, Sara, she told herself. He knows what he does to you. He knows, he knows . . .

'Sara.'

She looked at him helplessly. What was reality and what was illusion?

'What do you want to believe, Sara?'

She held back as he gathered her into his arms. But when his mouth closed hungrily on hers, as he drew her into the fierceness of his embrace, when she felt the power of his need for her, she moaned softly and swayed against him.

'Sara,' he said again, and she knew that she was lost.

CHAPTER EIGHT

RISING from the St Lawrence River in brightly lit splendour, the city of Montreal glittered in the chill dark of the ice-bound night. Sara had hoped for a glimpse of the Canadian city by daylight, but sunset came early in the northern winter. By the time she and Peter had crossed the border between the United States and Canada, night had fallen.

Not that she knew when they had passed that invisible line. There were illegal ways to make the passage from the soil of one nation to the other. Peter, of course, knew just how to find them . . .

It was he who ended their dizzying kiss before the fire, clasping her shoulders gently and putting her from him.

'Get some rest,' he said softly. 'I have work to do.'

It had taken a moment for her to focus on what he was saying. 'Work? What kind of——?'

'I want to check that Range Rover. Thompson always took good care of Grandfather's cars. With luck, the Rover will still run.'

Sara nodded. The Bronco had barely made it this far. Besides, the police would be looking for it by now. She knew how investigations went. There would be bulletins out everywhere; Peter would be the subject of an intense manhunt.

She sank down on the couch after he left the room, and stared into the fire. Had he told her the truth about the theft? He was only making things worse—he had stolen a car, he had certainly violated the terms of his parole . . .

Aren't you leaving something out, Sara? He abducted you.

And yet here she sat, unguarded and unfettered, waiting for his return. But what else could she do? There was no way out of this place on foot. She couldn't run, even if she wanted to. Even if she wanted to . . .

The sound of the door closing woke her. She sat up quickly, disorientated, and then she saw Peter crossing the room towards her, his arms laden with jackets and leather boots. He smiled at her.

'Did you have a good sleep?'

Sara nodded. 'Yes,' she said, although it wasn't true; she felt more tired than she had before, and her mind was filled with the smoky memories and fragmented dreams. 'Is the car all right?'

'It's purring like a kitten. Here,' he said, handing her a pair of knee-high boots, 'see if these fit.'

The boots were tight, but she managed to pull them on. 'They're fine,' she said, and she looked up at him. 'Are we leaving now?'

Peter nodded. 'I'll need daylight for the border crossing.'

The border crossing. Sara stared at him. Why hadn't she thought of that sooner? He would never make it into Canada. Even if the Customs officials hadn't been alerted, you needed papers of some kind to cross the border, didn't you? A birth certificate, a voter's card, something.

Peter's eyes narrowed. 'Sara? What is it?'

'Nothing,' she said. *They'll catch you, Peter.*

'Are you sure? You look upset.'

'No, I—these boots are small, that's all. They pinch a little.' *They'll catch you and I'll be free.*

'Sara.' He cupped her face in his hands. Slowly, her

eyes lifted to his. 'Don't be afraid, Sara. Nothing's going to happen to you. You have my word.'

Their eyes met and held, and then Sara swallowed. 'You—you won't get across the border,' she had heard herself say. 'You'll never make it through Customs.'

A smile, shadowed and mysterious, flickered across his face. 'Is that what you want?'

She swallowed again. 'I—I——'

Peter's lips brushed hers in a light kiss. 'It's all right, Sara.'

Now, as they drove through Montreal, she wondered again whether his whispered assurance had dealt with her uncertainty, or the possible danger waiting at the border. She had underestimated him, of course. He had never intended to enter Canada legally. He knew of an old dirt road that wound through the forest, a narrow track bootleggers had used more than sixty years before to run whiskey into the States during Prohibition. It had taken them safely from one country to the other . . .

She looked up as Peter pulled to the kerb and cut the engine. They were parked on a dark street. A sign opposite winked its crimson message into the night. 'Exotic Dancers', it read. 'Live and Lovely.'

Peter turned towards her and took hold of her hands. 'Listen to me, Sara.' His voice was low; there was a kind of urgency in it that made her pulse quicken. 'We're going to take a walk.'

She looked from the blinking sign to him. 'Here?'

He nodded. 'Yes. This is where I bid *adieu* to Peter Saxon, the man the police are looking for.'

Her head tilted to the side. 'I don't understand. How——?'

'Frenchy Nolan was my cellmate for a while. He said to look him up if I ever got to Montreal.' His eyes met hers, and a quick smile tilted at the corners of his mouth. 'I doubt if this is the kind of neighbourhood you're used to. Just remember to stay close beside me, and let me do the talking. All right?'

She drew in her breath. 'Yes.'

Peter smiled. 'Good girl. Now, come on. Let's play at being tourists out slumming.'

A frigid wind from the ice-choked river whipped at them as they got out of the car. Sara's glance fell to the floor in the rear, where a carelessly draped blanket concealed the tool-box. What if someone broke into the car and stole it? Peter seemed to know what she was thinking. The pressure of his arm around her waist urged her forward.

'There's no other way,' he said softly.

Their footsteps echoed along the pavement. The street they were on was tawdry, a sharp contrast to the others they had seen. Shops and bars advertised adult entertainment; signs offered artistic and discreet tattoos. The sharp smell of beer and cheap whiskey hung like a pall in the cold air.

Suddenly, Peter came to a stop. His arm tightened around her.

'Here we go,' he said softly. 'The Pink Pussycat Lounge.'

Sara looked up at the pulsing pink neon sign above the door. 'Does your friend own this place or something?'

His lips drew away from his teeth. 'Or something,' he said, and then he drew in his breath. 'OK, Sara, just remember what I said. Keep quiet, no matter what happens.'

The tavern was almost as dark as the street. The mingled smells of cigarettes and beer soaked the overheated air. Music spilled from a juke-box in one corner, flooding the room with the beat of drums and the wail of amplified guitars.

It was not a busy night at the Pink Pussycat. Wooden booths stood shadowed and unused against the wall. Peter paused in the doorway, and then his hand spread on the curve of Sara's hip, the press of his fingers firm and reassuring. They began walking slowly towards the far end of the bar.

Heads swivelled towards them, and men's eyes, hard and empty, appraised them. The few women Sara could see all had the same over-painted look, and turned away after a quick, bored glance.

'Look straight ahead, Sara,' Peter murmured. 'Don't make eye-contact with anyone.'

The bartender, a burly man with a flattened nose, looked them over dispassionately when they reached the stained mahogany bar.

'Something I can do for you people?'

Peter smiled easily. 'Yeah. You can tell Frenchy an old friend wants to see him.'

'And who says he wants to see you, pal?'

'Just tell him his New York room-mate says "hello".'

The man's eyes slid to Sara. 'I'll see if he's here.'

Moments later, they were ushered into a back room. As the door swung shut behind them, a fat man with a toothpick drooping from the corner of his mouth rose from behind a desk and held his hand out to Peter.

'Saxon,' he said with a grin, 'what the hell are you doing here?'

Peter grasped the outstretched hand. 'Looking for you, Nolan. What else would bring me to a such a dump?'

Both men smiled, and then the fat man sat down and leaned back in his chair. 'So,' he said, tonguing the toothpick to the other side of his mouth, 'you had a busy day yesterday.'

Sara felt Peter's muscles tense. 'Meaning?'

Nolan laughed, and tilted his chair back on two legs. 'Come on, old buddy, don't be modest. It was on the TV. They say you made quite a haul.'

Peter shrugged. 'You know how it goes,' he said casually. 'Everybody talks big.'

The fat man grinned. 'Five million bucks is pretty big, Saxon.'

'It won't be worth five cents if I don't find a way out of here,' Peter said. 'I have buyers waiting, but——'

'But you gotta get to them.' Nolan's small eyes narrowed thoughtfully. 'You want I should help you out, for old time's sake?' The toothpick rolled across his thick lips. 'I might be interested, for a cut of the merchandise. How's that sound?'

Sara drew in her breath. Was that why Peter had come here? Was he going to sell the jewels? Had that been his plan all along?

The pressure of his hand on her waist warned her to keep silent. 'No can do, Frenchy,' he said, after a pause. 'This was a contract job. There are big people involved. I don't deliver, and I'm dead.'

The fat man's eyes grew cold. 'Yeah, I know how it goes, old buddy.'

'What I need are papers. A passport. A birth certificate. A driver's licence. You know the stuff I mean.'

Nolan looked at Sara, and an oily smile spread over his face. 'I suppose this is Miss Sara Mitchell, hmm?' His glance went to Peter's arm, curved tightly around Sara's waist. 'They said you forced the lady to go with you, Saxon.'

Sara flushed beneath the fat man's knowing gaze. Beside her, Peter shrugged his shoulders.

'I told you they exaggerate, Nolan,' he said. 'Now,

how about those papers?'

The fat man spat the toothpick into his hand, and his pudgy fingers closed around it.

'Sure,' he said jovially, 'no problem, Saxon. Come back tomorrow and I'll have some names.'

'I need them tonight.'

The other man laughed. 'Yeah, I'll bet you do. But it's not that easy. I got to make some calls, check around—it's got to be tomorrow.'

'How much will this set me back, Nolan?' Peter's teeth flashed in a smile. 'I don't have much ready cash.'

Frenchy Nolan threw his head back and laughed. 'Hell, with that stash, who's worried about money?'

The men shook hands, and Sara and Peter started towards the door. With his hand on the knob, Peter stopped and turned around.

'By the way,' he said casually, 'how hot am I here?'

Nolan grinned. 'You'll make it to tomorrow, pal. New York's sitting in the middle of a snowstorm. The cops lost your trail—by the time they pick it up again, you and the lady will be in sunny Rio.'

'Right. Until tomorrow.'

As they made their way back through the tavern and towards the door, Sara started to speak, but Peter shook his head almost imperceptibly. They were inside the Range Rover, pulling away from the kerb, before he turned to her.

'Well, at least there's some good news,' he said. 'The storm's bought me a couple of days. The car park where I left the rental car is probably buried under two feet of snow. They won't dig it out until Monday.'

'Can that man really get you new identification papers?'

Peter shrugged. 'Yeah, if he wanted to.'

She nodded thoughtfully. 'So that's what you meant

when you talked about saying goodbye to . . .' She paused as what he had said registered. '*If* he wanted to? But he told you to come back tomorrow. He said——'

'Nolan's going to double-cross me.'

Her heart thumped wildly. 'You mean, he's going to call the police?'

He laughed. 'Hell, no, not the cops. He's going to take the jewels for himself. I tried to protect us by pretending I had buyers waiting, but it didn't work.'

'Then—then we can't go back there.'

We. We can't go back there.

'No, we can't.' He tapped his fingers on the steering wheel. 'There's got to be some other way.'

Sara looked at him. 'What other way? We're not even citizens of this country, Peter. We have American plates on the car, we have no passports or birth certificates. If anyone should stop us, we——'

Sara broke off in confusion. *Us. We.* Why did she keep doing that? They weren't in this together . . .

Peter reached across the seat, and clasped her hand in his. 'They aren't looking for us yet—not here, anyway. There's still time.' He smiled, and she thought she had never seen anyone look so weary in her life. 'What I need is a decent meal and a night's sleep. I can't think straight any more.'

'Will you drive back to Indian Lake?'

He shook his head. 'No, that would be crazy. I'm better off here. I just don't like the idea of staying in the city. There are too many strange faces, too many dark corners——' Suddenly, he looked across the car and smiled. 'Have you ever stayed in Canada before, Sara?'

The question took her by surprise. 'Me?' She shook her head and laughed. 'I've never been anywhere,' she said, 'unless you count Boston and New York.'

Peter squeezed her hand lightly in his. 'Well, the

night's still young,' he said. 'Suppose we take a look at a bit of Montreal.'

She thought, at first, that he was joking. But he wasn't; he turned the car down one street and then another, parking finally in a car park near a sign that read *'Métro'*.

Peter reached behind him and dug out a plaid wool cap. 'Here,' he said, 'tuck your hair up under that.' He pulled a knitted cap on his head, and added a pair of pale, tinted sunglasses. 'Well,' he said finally, 'it's not the world's best disguise, but it'll do.'

Then, carrying the tool-box as casually as if it contained nothing more than wrenches and screwdrivers, he took her hand and led her down a flight of steps.

Sara knew what *'métro'* meant: she expected an underground transit system. What she found was *la ville souterraine,* a sprawling city beneath a city—plazas and fountains, boutiques and cafés—all linked together. No wonder the frigid streets had seemed deserted, she thought, as she stared at the crowded mall. Montrealers had gone below ground for the winter.

She hesitated as he began to draw her forward. 'Aren't you taking an awful chance?'

He shook his head. 'We're just two more anonymous faces in a sea of shoppers.'

'Yes, but——'

'We have to make some purchases, Sara. Tooth-brushes. Combs. Shaving things.' He laughed softly and drew her close to his side. 'That sweater.' She stared into a shop-window filled with cashmere sweaters in dazzling shades of blue. Peter bent his head to hers. 'Do you see it? The one in the back.'

He was looking at an indigo sweater that looked as soft as a kitten's fur. Sara smiled and shook her head.

'It's lovely. But it's far too expensive. And the colour's too deep for me . . . Peter? Peter, what are you——?'

He tugged her into the shop after him. In moments, the sweater, delicate as gossamer, had been packed in a pale peach box, and tucked into a bag.

'Come again,' the shop-girl called after them. Sara, her face flushed with delight, gazed up at Peter as he led her through the crowded mall.

'Are you crazy?' she whispered. 'So much money. I've never spent that on a dress, let alone a sweater.'

He smiled at her. 'I can hardly wait to see you wearing it. The blue's almost the colour of your eyes.'

She stared at him. 'No,' she said quickly, 'my eyes are too dark. They're not——'

He stopped suddenly, and looked down at her. The crowd flowed around them like the sea. 'Midnight blue, sweet Sara.' His voice caressed her. 'That's the colour of your eyes. Hasn't anyone ever told you that?'

Heat flooded her body and centred in her cheeks. She shook her head.

'No,' she whispered.

Peter's eyes grew dark. 'Sara . . .' A laughing group of teenaged girls jostled them, and he let out his breath. 'Come on,' he said gruffly, 'we're making a traffic jam.'

He clasped her hand, and they began walking again. Moments later, they stopped at a shop selling sporting goods. Peter bought a knapsack, then, returning to the concourse and stopping at an empty bench, he calmly transferred the jewels from the tool-box to the knapsack, which he slung over his shoulder. The tool-box disappeared beneath the bench as he turned, took her hand, and walked away.

Sara was dumbfounded. In the midst of hundreds of

people, no one had paid them any attention.

'You're not really going to carry the jewels in that, are you?'

Peter grinned. 'Just make sure I haven't left a necklace hanging out, will you, please? Now, let's see what else we need.'

They ended up with an armful of packages—toiletries as well as sweaters and jeans. Finally, Peter paused outside a small café and peered into its candle-lit depths.

'Last stop,' he said, 'and then we'll call it a night and get some sleep. How does this suit you?'

We'll get some sleep . . . Sara managed a smile. 'Fine.'

They took a table in the rear of the little room. Peter was relaxed and smiling, but she noticed that he chose a chair which put his back to the wall and gave him a clear view of the open doorway. He ordered for them both, watching with obvious pleasure as Sara tucked into her meal.

'I'll never eat all this,' she said. But she did, from the green salad to the *steak au poivre* to the gâteau, and then she sat back and sighed.

'I think I just made a pig of myself,' she said with a little smile. 'My mother would never have approved.'

Peter leaned his elbows on the table. 'No?'

Sara shook her head. 'No.' She laughed softly. 'I can't believe this.'

His eyebrows rose. 'That you just made a pig of yourself?' he asked innocently.

She smiled. 'You know what I mean, Peter. Here we are, sitting in Montreal, with a bag filled with jewels on the chair between us——'

He reached across the table and put his hand over hers. 'We're safe enough for now, Sara. And I'll think of something for tomorrow.'

'I wasn't thinking that,' she said. 'I was thinking that it was crazy, but I feel——'

Her words tumbled into confused silence. Goodness, what was wrong with her? She had almost told him she was happy, that she was having the time of her life.

She had to be mad. But it was true—she felt alive in a way she never had before. Colours were sharper, scents crisper. She looked around the candle-lit room, at the other diners, and she thought suddenly of how commonplace their lives must be.

Peter had tried to explain what it was like to live on the edge. Was that what she felt? Had danger quickened her senses?

'Sara.'

His voice was low, but it cut through her tangled thoughts. Her head came up sharply, and she looked at him. The expression on his face made her breath catch.

'What's wrong, Peter?'

'We have to leave now,' he said. He rose slowly, and dropped some bills on the table. 'OK, I want you to stand. Easy. Easy, Sara, don't hurry. That's right. No, don't look away from me. Smile at me. Good. Now, come on, take my hand.'

Could she manage to walk? Her legs felt as if they were going to buckle. And she couldn't breathe very well. But Peter was holding her hand, leading her from the café and into the mall.

Oh, hell!

She saw the policeman just as they reached the steps leading to the street. He was so close that she had only to reach out to touch him. Her heart pounded in her ears, her palms grew damp. Peter, she thought, Peter . . .

But Peter was talking to her, smiling and nodding as if they were just two people out for the evening, and finally, they were past the policeman and on the street.

She gasped for air as she stumbled into the cold winter night. 'Peter,' she whispered.

His arms closed around her. 'It's all right,' he murmured. 'Sweet Sara, it's all right now.'

'Are you sure?'

He held her trembling body close to his. 'You were wonderful.'

She leaned back in his embrace, and looked up at him. 'Are you sure he didn't notice us?'

He nodded. 'I'm sure.' He smiled into her eyes. 'But someone will, if we stand here and turn into chunks of ice.'

She made a sound that was supposed to be a laugh. 'OK, then. What do we do next?'

He unlocked the Range Rover and lifted her inside. 'We head north, into the Laurentian Mountains.' The engine turned over, and he edged into traffic. 'It's a big winter resort area—there are scores of hotels and cabins, and heaven knows how many skiers.' He smiled, almost apologetically. 'It's all I can think of at the moment.'

Two hours later, Sara stood inside a small chalet, watching through the window as Peter pulled the car around the side and tucked it into a small copse of trees. He got out, walked to the narrow road that led to the chalet, and peered towards the trees. When he entered the chalet, he nodded.

'OK,' he said, tossing their packages on the couch, 'that should do it. You can't see the car until you get really close. Not that anyone's going to be checking, but there's no sense taking chances.'

He switched on the lights, and she blinked in the sudden glare. They were in a handsome living-room with a stone fireplace. Dark beams crossed the ceiling.

There was a door beyond, and a canopied bed just visible past it.

'How are you at haircuts?'

She stared at him. 'At what?'

'Haircuts.' He pulled off his jacket, then walked through the room, drawing the heavy curtains at each window. 'I want to change my appearance as much as I can.' He ran his fingers through his dark hair, and then touched his moustache. 'I can't do much with the specifics, but a shave and a haircut ought to help a little. So what do you say, Miss Mitchell? How would you like to give me a trim?'

She nodded. 'I'll try. But I've never——'

Peter's smile curved softly. 'That's good, Sara. I want to be the first.'

Her eyes met his as he moved towards her, and suddenly she felt the same dizzying rush of excitement she had felt in the mall. He stopped beside her, cupped her face in his hands, and smiled.

'The next man who kisses you will be a man without a moustache.' He bent to her, and his mouth took hers in a deep, sweet kiss that left her breathless. 'That's just so you'll have a basis for comparison,' he said, and then he let her go.

She watched as he started towards the bedroom. At the last minute, he turned and tossed something bright and metallic to her. She reached out automatically, and caught the keys to the Range Rover.

Sara's eyes met Peter's, and he smiled. 'Leave them on the table near the door,' he said. 'I don't think anything's going to happen, but, just in case we have to move fast, I don't want to waste time searching.' He smiled again as he read the question in her eyes. 'You won't run out on me, sweet Sara. We both know that.'

She stared after him as the bathroom door opened,

then closed after him, and then she sank down on the nearest chair. Her fingers curled around the keys, until the sharp metal edges pressed into her flesh.

What a fool she had been! It wasn't danger that had filled her with such fierce joy and elation.

It was Peter Saxon.

And he knew it.

CHAPTER NINE

DAMN him! Damn him, damn him, damn . . .

'You won't run out on me, sweet Sara. We both know that.'

What an absolute fool she had been! Tears of anger rose in her eyes, and she blinked them away. She could hear the sound of water running in the bathroom and, over that, Peter Saxon's cheerful, off-key whistle. He sounded as if he were a man getting ready to go to work in the morning, instead of one on the run from the law.

But then, why should he be upset? Everything was going along just fine. Oh, his Montreal contact hadn't panned out, but Peter was resourceful; he would find a way around that little snag. What mattered was that he had pulled off the jewel theft of the decade. And now, thanks to her, he was making good his escape.

'I didn't steal the Winstead jewels.'

That was what he'd said, and she'd been all too eager to believe him—never mind the facts. Never mind that Peter Saxon was a convicted thief, that he was the only person who had had access to the jewels, that she'd seen the tumble of glittering gems in the boot of his car with her very own eyes.

He had played her like a violin, damn him. Two days ago—an eternity ago—she'd recognised Saxon's game for what it was; she'd known he was manipulating her. Next to masterminding spectacular jewel thefts, taking advantage of women was probably what he did best.

He only took what a woman gladly offered, he'd said, but the arrogant son of a bitch knew how to make them offer everything! She cringed as she remembered how compassionate she'd been when he told her about his childhood—all lies, probably. And she didn't even want to think of how she'd helped him walk right past the policeman in the mall a little while ago. It was just too humiliating.

Her footsteps slowed, and she stared into the bedroom. The canopied bed seemed enormous, lurid despite the virginal white of its eyelet coverings. That was the setting for the next step in his plan. He'd seduced her into complicity; now he would seduce her into bed. And, by tomorrow morning, the pathetic spinster from Brookville would be his completely, ready to be led into the final step of the dance choreographed by the Devil and Peter Saxon.

'Sara?'

She turned towards the bathroom. The sound of running water had stopped, and the door stood ajar. Steam billowed through it, obscuring her view.

'Sara? I'm ready for that haircut.'

Her heart hammered in her throat. She had the keys to the Range Rover in her hand. All she had to do was step through the door and close it after her. That was the easiest thing.

But she couldn't do it. Not without losing her self-respect. If she was ever going to be able to look in the mirror without cringing, she had to tell Peter Saxon she knew what he was up to. She had to look him in the eye and tell him that she wasn't quite the naïve fool he thought, that his ugly little game wasn't going to work any more.

'Sara?'

She spun towards the sound of his voice, angry words on her lips. But the sight of him made the breath catch in her throat.

He stood in the bathroom doorway, naked to the waist except for a white towel draped casually across his shoulders. Drops of water gleamed in his hair and on his skin. She watched, hypnotised, as a droplet trickled lazily through the dark mat of hair on his chest, down his ribs to the ridged muscles on his abdomen, and then to his navel. Her glance fell lower, to the unbuttoned waistband of his corduroys, and then flew upward to his face.

'Well, what do you think? Do I look as naked as I feel?'

He grinned and touched his fingers to his upper lip. She realised for the first time that his moustache was gone. He looked younger, she thought, almost vulnerable. But still just as handsome. And just as dangerous.

His grin grew a little crooked as he waited for her to answer. 'It can't be that bad, Sara. Come on, what's the verdict?'

Sara lifted her chin. 'Life,' she said coolly.

Peter cocked his head. 'Life? What's that supposed to mean?'

'You asked what the verdict was,' she answered. 'And I'm telling you. Life. That's what any intelligent jury will give you.'

It pleased her to see his smile begin to dim. 'What are you talking about?'

She looked into his eyes. 'The jig's up,' she said. 'Isn't that what they used to say in old movies?'

His smile dimmed a little more. 'I'm going to have to learn not to leave you alone, Sara Mitchell. Every time I do . . .'

'. . . the spell wears off. Yes, I know. The only difference is that this time it's gone for good.'

His smile vanished. 'All right,' he said, putting his

hands on his hips, 'let's have it. What the hell's going on?'

Somehow, despite the staccato beat of her heart, she managed a careless shrug.

'You made a tactical error, Peter. I think the scientific term is counting one's chickens before they have hatched.'

His eyes narrowed. 'Meaning?'

'Meaning I finally remembered just what we were doing here.' Her eyes met his. '*You're* here because you stole five million dollars' worth of jewels——'

'Hell, are we back to that?'

'. . . and *I'm* here because you took me prisoner.'

'Sara, for heaven's sake, listen to me.'

'That's exactly what I did,' she said coldly. '"You won't run out on me, sweet Sara. We both know that."' she mimicked. 'You shouldn't have said that, Peter. But I guess you couldn't help yourself; you're so full of conceit that——'

He took a step towards her. 'Are you crazy?'

'Just stay away from me,' she said quickly. 'If you take another step, I'll——'

His lips drew back from his teeth. 'You'll what?' he asked softly. 'Come on, Sara, let's hear it. What will you do?'

She felt a flutter of fear. There had been a subtle change in him. His voice, the way he was looking at her, even the angle of his head, suddenly seemed menacing. But it was too late to back off now, even if she'd wanted to. And she didn't, not with the scent of victory in her nostrils.

She would tell him what she thought of him, and then leave him standing there, while she fled into the night.

The advantage was all hers. He was bare-footed and half-dressed, and it was probably not more than ten degrees outside and snowing.

She was still fully dressed. And she had the car keys in her hand.

She began moving towards the door, her eyes locked with his. 'You're really good, you know. I mean, you just about convinced me of your innocence.'

He shook his head impatiently. 'I *am* innocent. I told you——'

'Yes, you told me. That whole sad story about your father, and your brother, and how you couldn't face being locked up again.'

His mouth twisted. 'It's all true. I haven't lied to you about anything.'

'How pathetic I must seem to you. Sara Mitchell, naïve spinster, plain Jane——'

'Stop this nonsense!'

'"You won't run out on me, sweet Sara."' Her voice mocked his cruelly again, then broke. 'You've been using me from the start, you son of a bitch.'

Peter began walking towards her, his hand outstretched. 'Give me the car keys, Sara.'

His voice was cold. It sent a shudder up her spine, but she shook her head.

'Stay away from me.'

Her back was against the wall now; she reached out her hand and felt for the door. It had to be close. Yes! Yes, there it was. Her fingers slid across the jamb to the knob. If she could just . . .

'Sara. Look out!'

Something white flashed at her, and snapped inches from her eyes. She ducked her head and whirled away from it instinctively. Peter was on her instantly, swinging her into his arms and lifting her from the floor.

Sara slammed her hand against his shoulder. 'No,'

she cried, 'don't!'

Her heart felt as if it were going to explode as she struggled against him. The old Peter Saxon was back, the one who had kidnapped her on the ice-slicked road in Brookville. He shifted her in his arms and looked down at her, a quick smile tilting across his mouth, his eyes the colour of the night.

'Such an old trick, sweetheart,' he said. 'But it takes sharp reflexes to see it coming.'

The towel. He had taken the towel from his neck and snapped it towards her. That was all that had happened, but it had been enough. The advantage that had been hers was gone, along with her chance at freedom.

Panic rose in her throat. 'Let go of me,' she said. 'I'll scream if you——'

He laughed softly. 'Go on,' he whispered, his voice like silk, 'scream.' His arms tightened around her. 'The chalet's surrounded by forest, the wind's howling like a banshee—scream, and see what it gets you.'

Sara swallowed past the sharp taste of terror. 'I'm not afraid of you,' she said.

His eyes met hers. 'Aren't you?'

She swallowed again. 'N . . . no. I——'

His lips drew back from his teeth. 'Good. That makes it easier.'

She read his intention in his eyes, and she began to struggle wildly as he strode through the living-room towards the bedroom door, but it was impossible to wrench free. He was all hard muscle and harder determination; she beat at his shoulders and chest, but the blows meant no more to him than snowflakes falling on granite.

She grabbed the doorjamb as they went through, but her fingers slipped away uselessly. Peter kicked the door closed behind him. The canopied bed loomed ahead but, to Sara's amazement, he marched past it to the full-length mirror on the far side of the room. There, he dropped her to her feet, grasped her shoulders, and shoved her in front of him.

'Take a good look, Sara. Tell me what you see.'

She stared into the mirror. A wild-eyed woman, cheeks flushed, hair in loose disarray, looked back at her. Peter Saxon glowered behind her, dark and threatening.

Her heart thudded erratically. 'Don't make this worse than it already is. If you know what's good for you, you'll——'

'Answer the question.'

She stared at their images, and a flush rose to her cheeks. 'Do you want to hear me admit I'm afraid of you? All right, I am. Are you satisfied now? Is that——?'

His hand slid to her neck. She watched as his fingers covered the pulse beating wildly in the hollow of her throat.

'Do you know *why* you're afraid of me?' His voice was low and smoky. He bent his head towards hers, until she felt the press of his cheek against her hair, and the warmth of his breath on her cheek.

Why was it so hard to draw air into her lungs? Sara swallowed, then swallowed again.

'Of course,' she whispered. 'You're bigger than I am. Stronger.'

He laughed. 'And a hell of a lot meaner.' His smile fled, and he moved closer to her. She could feel the hard warmth of his body against hers. 'But that isn't the reason, is it?'

She drew a laboured breath. 'I don't know what you're talk——'

'The woman in the mirror knows,' he whispered. His

eyes met hers in the glass, and he smiled. 'I brought her to life. And that's what scares the hell out of you, Sara. It has from the minute we met.'

Her eyes widened. 'What? What are you——?'

'You've had her bottled up inside for so long that you almost destroyed her.' Peter smiled lazily. 'And then I came along.'

Sara laughed shakily. 'Did I say you were conceited? Hell, they haven't invented the word to describe you, Peter Saxon. You just can't accept the truth, can you? I've seen through your scheme. It's finished. You can't use me any——'

He spun her towards him. His hands cupped her face and lifted it to his.

'You talk too much, Sara,' he said, and his mouth dropped to hers in a passionate kiss.

She stood cold and rigid within his embrace, her lips unresponsive to the harsh demand of his. When he released her, she shook her head.

'You see? It won't work. I told you that. I——'

He caught her to him again, his hand tangling in the hair at the back of her head, the tension painful as he pulled her head back.

'Shut up,' he said with a raw savagery. 'Just shut the hell up, Sara.'

His mouth fell on hers again, in a kiss so filled with hunger and promise that it made her tremble. Something darker than fear sent the blood pounding through her veins. When finally he lifted his head, she drew a shuddering breath.

'What . . . what happened to all those boasts about never taking what a woman didn't gladly offer? Or was that all lies, too?'

His eyes met hers. 'You're the liar, Sara, not me.'

She tried to laugh, but the sound was no more than a

choked cry.

'I don't know what you're talking about.'

Peter smiled tightly. 'That little world you live in is so safe, isn't it? You can close your eyes and pretend . . .'

'You're crazy. I——'

'. . . and pretend it's real,' he said, drawing her more closely against him. 'But it isn't, Sara.' He drew in his breath. 'Life is what's real—it's the only reality there is. You just have to reach out, and it's yours.'

'Damn you, Peter Saxon.'

His hand slipped to her cheek. She felt the heat of it burn against her flesh. His thumb slid across her parted lips.

'Let go, just this once.' His voice dropped to a velvet whisper. 'Sweet Sara, let go and touch reality.'

'No,' she whispered, 'I don't . . .'

He held her face steady as he lowered his mouth to hers. Sara tensed herself for the demand of his kiss, but it was gentle and tender. He drew back and looked into her eyes for a long moment, and then he bent to her and kissed her again. When he drew away this time, she was trembling.

'Put your arms around me,' he said softly.

'Peter.' She whispered his name and closed her eyes. 'Don't,' she said, 'please, don't.'

'Do it.'

Slowly, reluctantly, she lifted her arms. She put her hands against his chest. The heat of his body was a cauldron against her palms.

'Put your arms around my neck, Sara.'

She held her breath as she moved her hands slowly up his chest, and linked them behind his neck. He made a sound she barely heard, something that was not quite a moan, and her lashes lifted from her cheeks.

The look on his face made her blood leap. Desire

blazed in the darkness of his eyes; a vein beat in his forehead.

'Peter.' The word was barely a whisper. 'Peter.'

He bent to her, and touched his mouth to her throat. Her head fell back as she felt the nip of his teeth at the pulse point of shoulder and neck.

'You smell like spring rain,' he said thickly. 'And you taste—you taste like honey.' She felt the rasp of his tongue against her skin, and her eyes fell closed again. 'I'm going to taste you everywhere, Sara. Your mouth, your eyelids, your throat . . .'

The dreams of a hundred nights bloomed within her, dreams her mind had always rejected in the cool light of dawn. Peter's hands moved over her, and her body sparked to life wherever his fingers stroked. She felt his mouth against her, heard him whisper words that were muffled by her skin, but she understood them just the same.

He wanted her, just as she wanted him. She had denied the truth to him and to herself from the beginning, but the time for denial was past.

Peter Saxon was the man she had waited for all her life. He was everything she had wanted, and everything she had feared.

He was life. He was reality. And she would not let this moment slip away.

She moved against him, and wound her fingers into the thick hair at the back of his head.

'Peter,' she sighed.

The sound of her voice seemed to inflame him. He whispered her name as he buried his face in her hair and swept her up into his arms. In a few quick strides he crossed the room, and sank down with her into the softness of the canopied bed, drawing her into the curve of his shoulder as he bent over her and kissed her deeply.

Her lips parted beneath the pressure of his; his tongue stroked hers. His hand moved over her with tantalising slowness, learning the length of her leg, the curve of her hip, the thrust of her breasts.

He was talking to her, whispering to her, but she couldn't understand him. Ablaze with a thousand new sensations, Sara could only feel. But it was enough. Peter's hands and mouth and body spoke more eloquently than words; she understood their message, and answered with her own. Her arms tightened around him, and she sighed his name against his mouth.

He pushed her sweater up, and she gasped as she felt the heated press of his hand against her flesh. His fingertips were roughened; the feel of them moving against her sent a flood of warmth racing to her loins. When his hand closed over her naked breast, she moaned softly.

No man had ever touched her like this before. No man had ever kissed her this way, or whispered these things to her. She was alive and eager for what only Peter Saxon could offer.

'Sara,' he whispered. Her eyes opened slowly, and focused on his face. It was drawn with desire. A surge of excitement shot through her. 'Come fly like an eagle,' he said softly, and he pulled her sweater over her head and tossed it aside.

She trembled as he looked at her, his eyes hot on her naked breasts. She felt her nipples bud even before he touched her.

'Beautiful Sara,' he whispered, 'my sweet love.'

She caught her bottom lip between her teeth as he reached out to her and ran his hand lightly along her skin, his fingers defining the shadow of ribs, grazing the soft underswell of breast, until finally he cupped her flesh in his palm. Her lashes fell to her cheeks as his thumb brushed across the nipple; the sensation his touch aroused was so sharp and sweet that she felt it in her bones.

His mouth moved over her flesh, his tongue leaving a trail of radiance from her shoulder to the hollow between her breasts, until, at last, his lips closed over the waiting nipple.

'Peter . . .' It was all she could manage to whisper as she held him to her.

All sensation was centred in the place where his mouth and her body met. Nothing had prepared her for this feeling; nothing could equal it, she thought—and then she felt the touch of his hand on her belly, over her corduroy trousers. His hand stroked, gentled, finally cupped the soft mounded centre of her, and Sara felt waves of heat begin to sing through her body.

'Help me,' he whispered, and she raised her hips to him as he slid down her trousers. She watched his face as he pulled the last bit of clothing from her. His eyes moved over her like a caress. 'You're beautiful, Sara,' he said, and, for the first time in her life, she knew it was true.

'I want to see you, too,' she whispered.

He smiled and touched her cheek. 'Yes,' he said, and he rose to his feet. Their eyes held as he unzipped his trousers and stepped free of them.

His body was the colour of new wheat. Long ridges of muscle lay coiled beneath his skin. He was a dizzying blend of virility and beauty, and Sara felt herself quicken at the sight of him. She raised her arms to him, and drew him down beside her.

His mouth met hers. He kissed her, tender little kisses that coaxed her lips apart, until, with sudden ferocity, he gathered her to him and rolled her beneath him.

'Sara,' he whispered, 'sweet, sweet Sara.'

His hands and mouth were everywhere, the silken brush of his tongue augmented by the heated rasp of his fingertips. She cried out as he ran his hand over her belly and into the damp delta between her thighs. The stroke of his fingers electrified her, but when she felt the touch of his lips at her navel, then at the secret of her womanhood, she drew in her breath.

'Don't,' she said, 'oh . . .'

Peter caught her hands in his. 'Yes,' he said, 'yes, sweet Sara. Let me taste you. Let me.'

The imprint of his kiss sent her spiralling upwards through glimmering bands of light. She was caught in a rainbow; the brilliance of it dazzled her senses. Tears rose behind her closed eyelids and rolled down her cheeks.

When Peter finally knelt between her legs, and thrust into her body, she felt the pulsebeat of the universe quicken. And then they were travelling together to a place of shimmering crystal radiance, where colour became sound, became heat, became sensation.

'Sara,' he said hoarsely. Poised on the brink of eternity, Sara whispered Peter's name. He kissed her, the kiss tasting of the passion he had aroused within her, and then she closed her arms around him and they were one with the gods.

She awoke in the dark, small hours of the night, safe and warm in Peter's arms.

'Did I wake you?' he whispered. 'I didn't mean to; I only wanted to pull up the covers.'

Sara smiled into the darkness and snuggled closer to him. 'I'm warm enough,' she said sleepily. 'Aren't you?'

He laughed softly. 'Shameless wench,' he said,

drawing the blankets over them both. Seconds passed, and then he rose up above her on one elbow. 'Sara?'

She sighed. 'Mmm.'

'I told you the truth, love. I didn't steal the Winstead jewels.'

Her eyes opened and she looked at him. In the dark, his face was shadowed.

'It doesn't matter,' she whispered, and she knew that was the truth.

He smiled, and caught her hand in his. 'Thank you for saying that,' he said, pressing a kiss into her palm. 'But I didn't steal them, Sara. Someone just wanted it to look as if I had.'

Sara sat up against the pillows. The blankets fell to her waist. 'But why? What would be the sense?'

Peter reached out and switched on the lamp. 'Remember when I emptied the jewels from the tool-box into the knapsack?' She nodded. 'Well, it was the first time I took a good look at them.' He ran his fingers through his tousled hair, then looked at her. 'The best pieces are missing, Sara. The tiara, the diamond and emerald necklace, the matching ring and bracelet——'

She stared at him. 'But—but what does it mean?'

Peter smiled crookedly. 'It means,' he said slowly, 'that I think I know who set me up.' He reached out and ran the backs of his fingers lazily along her throat.

Sara's eyes widened. 'Who?'

His fingertips grazed her breast. 'I think I know why, too.'

'Tell me, Peter.'

His eyes darkened as he bent to her. 'I will,' he said softly. His lips brushed hers, and she felt the gentle pressure of his teeth. 'In the morning. There are more important things to do now.'

And, as his arms closed around her, Sara knew he was right.

CHAPTER TEN

'SIMON WINSTEAD? You think the jeweller stole his own jewels, and made it look as if you'd done it?' Sara stared at Peter across the tray of croissants and coffee that sat in the middle of the canopied bed. 'But why?'

He reached towards her and brushed a tousled strand of hair from her eyes. 'You are the most persistent woman.' She was sitting cross-legged, dressed only in his flannel shirt. His eyes moved over her bare legs, paused at her breasts, and came to rest on her mouth. 'We could talk about this later, you know. Say, in an hour or two.'

Sara smiled, and caught his hand in hers. 'And you,' she said softly, 'are impossible. Here I am, trying to be serious——'

'Here I am, trying to make love to you——' Peter returned her smile, then leaned across the breakfast tray and kissed her. 'Mmm,' he said, 'coffee with cream and sugar. Just the way I like it.'

'Peter, please. You said you'd tell me about the Maharanee of Gadjapur's jewels.'

He sighed. 'And I did. I told you Winstead's the thief, not me.'

'Yes,' she said impatiently, 'but why would he steal his own property? And how? It doesn't make any sense.'

Peter swung his legs to the floor. 'The "how" is easy. Remember those power blackouts? We all assumed they were due to the storm, but Winstead could have rigged them. I'd even suggested he arrange some sort of power

145

back-up, because of the house's remote location, but he shrugged it off. And it would have been easy enough to open the boot of my car and plant the jewels.' He shrugged his shoulders. 'I left the keys in it, remember, so the valet could move it if he had to.'

Sara nodded. 'I just don't understand why he would involve you. He didn't need you there just so he could take his own property out of his own safe.'

Peter smiled ruefully. 'He did if he was going to get away with the scam he'd rigged. Who would suspect the respected Simon Winstead of theft if I were around?'

'But why did he keep some of the jewels?'

'Not some, love. The best. The most expensive.' He reached to the tangled clothing beside the bed, and began separating it. 'When the police caught me, they would have accused me of having already sold those pieces off. Meanwhile, they would be safe and sound in Winstead's safe.'

Scepticism showed on Sara's face. 'Not in his safe, Peter. Why on earth would he keep them there?'

'Because that's the safest place for them, that's why. Who would look for stolen jewels in the safe they were supposedly stolen from?'

It was a plan as simple, yet as complex, as any Sara could imagine. And, the more she considered it, the more sense it made.

'Yes, but why would he do it? The man's worth a fortune.'

Peter's eyebrows rose. 'That's what they say, but who knows? Maybe he blew it all on the stock market. Maybe he made some bad business moves. Maybe he just likes the idea of screwing the insurance company.'

Sara nodded. 'To the tune of—what—a million dollars?'

Peter smiled. 'Three million, at least. And the

insurance company pays him that much again——'

'. . . because they won't be able to recover the jewels you supposedly stole.'

'Right. He gets the jewels and the money, I get put away, and he's home free.'

'But—he must have known you would figure it out.'

Peter laughed. 'Come on, Sara. Suppose I tried telling this story to the cops. Do you really think they would believe it? I have no credibility, but I sure as hell have the jewels. It's an open and shut case.'

Sara smiled at him. 'Not any more, it isn't. All we have to do is call my boss and——'

'Sara.' Peter's hand closed over hers as she reached for the phone. 'We can't do that.'

'Don't be silly. All you have to do is tell Chief Garrett what you just told me. And then he'll . . . he'll . . .'

He nodded. 'Exactly. Even if he believed you, what could he do? He'd need a search warrant to get into Winstead's safe. And no court's going to order a warrant based on a fairy-tale spun by a convicted felon like me.'

Sara sighed deeply. 'You're right,' she admitted. Her eyes met his and she gave him a quick smile. 'I just—I don't think of you that way, Peter. It's impossible for me to think of you as a—as a thief.'

A smile twisted across his mouth. 'Is it?'

She nodded. 'Yes. The more I know you, the more difficult it is.'

Peter ran his hand along her cheek. 'I never gave a damn what anyone thought of me—until now. Now—I wish I could go back and . . .' He drew in his breath. 'But it's not possible. I am what I am, and I did what I had to do . . .'

His words trailed away. Sara took his hand in hers and held it tightly.

'Of course you did,' she said. 'I understand that.'

'No,' he said softly. 'you don't.'

'I do,' she insisted. 'You had no choice but to run. You're right, no one would have believed you hadn't stolen the jewels.'

It seemed to Sara that all the sadness in the world was in his smile.

'Which brings us full circle. There's no way out for me.'

Sara shook her head. 'There's *got* to be. Can't you think of anything?'

Peter laughed softly. 'Sure. All I have to do is drive back to Brookville, break into Winstead's house, open the safe, and find the missing jewels.'

'Could you do that?' she asked softly. 'Break into the house and into the safe without getting caught?'

He grinned. 'Modesty compels me to say "no", but honesty demands the truth. Of course I could. I supervised the electronic systems for Winstead, remember? I'd need some things——'

'What things?'

He sighed and got to his feet. 'Things,' he said vaguely. 'Nothing I couldn't pick up in any hardware store.' He looked at her and shook his head. 'It's just a pipe-dream, Sara. Even if I did something that crazy, what would be the point?'

'You would find the missing jewels, the ones that would prove Winstead set you up.'

Peter shook his head. 'Sorry, sweetheart. They would simply accuse me of putting them back in the safe. It wouldn't work. Hell, I'd need a gold-plated witness if I——'

'You have a witness.' Sara stood up and walked towards him. 'You have me.'

Peter stared at her. 'What are you talking about?'

Her eyes shone with eagerness. 'If I were with you when you opened the safe, I could testify that the tiara and the emeralds were already there, and that you had never had them. Chief Garrett would believe me, Peter. He trusts me. He——' A slow flush rose to her cheeks. 'Why are you looking at me that way?'

He took her in his arms and kissed her, and then he smiled at her. 'Thank you for the offer, sweetheart, but——'

'Peter, please. I want to do it. Don't you see? I want to do something to help you.'

'No. It's insane. It could be dangerous.'

'So is life,' she said. Her eyes met his. 'But that's what makes it exciting. Isn't that what you told me?'

Peter's eyes darkened. 'If you want excitement,' he said, 'I can give you all you need.'

He gathered her to him, moulding her body to his. Her mouth opened to his; she felt the heated press of his aroused body against her, and the slow, sweet passion he had unleashed began to unwind deep within her.

'Please,' she whispered, 'let me help you.'

He swung her into his arms, and looked down at her. 'Has anyone ever told you that you talk too much?' he asked thickly, and then he lowered her to the bed, and the room and reality spun away.

Hours later, they were riding south towards Brookville in the Range Rover. It had taken all morning for Sara to talk Peter into going back; now, as he sat silent and tense beside her, she felt her own anxiety mounting.

Peter's mood had deteriorated as the miles sped by. She'd been surprised, at first, remembering how charged with excitement flirting with danger made him—until she realised that this was more than that.

This was a game played for the highest stakes of all.

Freedom.

The closer they got to the scene of the theft, the greater the risk he would be captured. And if he were, he would be locked behind bars.

'I thought I'd die in there.'

A car shot by them, horn blaring into the night. Peter muttered an obscenity.

'Go on,' he said, 'kill yourself, you stupid idiot.'

He was like a coiled spring! Sara cleared her throat.

'You're only doing forty, Peter. That's why he passed you.'

He glared at her, his fingers tightening on the steering wheel. 'Who's driving this car, Sara, you or me?'

She looked at him in bewilderment. 'I was only——'

'Yes, I know what you were "only". You were——' Suddenly, he drew in his breath and slapped his hand against the wheel. 'Hell,' he said softly, 'I must be crazy.' His foot pressed down on the accelerator and the car moved ahead. 'Too slow is just as bad as too fast for calling attention to yourself.'

'You're tired, that's all. We've been on the road half the night.'

He shook his head. 'Don't make excuses for me,' he said irritably. 'It doesn't change the fact that I made a mistake.' He glanced at her again, and then looked back to the road. 'And I damned well can't afford to make mistakes. Not any more.'

Sara put her hand on his. 'I wasn't making excuses for you. I only meant that I know you're under a lot of pressure and——'

His voice cut across hers. 'I can't believe I let you talk me into this crazy plan.'

Her hand fell away from his. 'It's not crazy,' she said quickly.

Too quickly, Sara, she thought. Where's all that

conviction you felt earlier? But she knew where it was; it had slipped away along with Peter's confidence. He was her strength, and, if he had doubts about their plan succeeding, it was doomed to failure.

'Of course it's crazy,' he said. 'We're going to break into the Winstead house. A thousand things could go wrong.'

'Nothing will go wrong,' she said, with a certainty she didn't feel. 'You said you could get into that security system with your eyes closed.'

He scowled. 'If it's the same system. If Winstead hasn't moved the jewels. If we don't run into the police. If——'

She looked at him, surprised at the sharpness in his voice. 'You never mentioned any of those things this morning.'

His jaw thrust forward. 'There are a dozen possibilities I didn't mention. That doesn't mean I'm not aware of them. Anything might go wrong in a caper like this.'

Sara hesitated while she searched for words that would calm his fears.

'There's a risk,' she said finally. 'OK, I figured that. I——'

'You're damned right there is.'

'Talk about role-reversal,' she said with a forced little laugh. 'I thought you were the one who lived for risks.'

Peter looked at her, and then at the road. 'People change, Sara. Maybe I've finally figured out that sometimes the risk is greater than the reward.'

She bit down on her lip. There was no need to ask what he meant. He was thinking of prison again, she knew. She ached to tell him she would do anything to protect him—but there was nothing she could think of, except what they had planned—and, the more she thought of breaking into the Winstead house, the more dangerous it seemed.

But what other choice was there? If they had stayed in Canada, sooner or later the authorities would have picked up their trail. Still, that might have been safer than what they were doing.

A cold knot settled in her gut. She was leading him into the very heart of danger. Her plan, so clever and daring when she had suggested it that morning, suddenly seemed impossible.

'Peter,' she said, turning towards him, 'listen to me——'

'There's our exit,' he said, swinging the wheel to the right. 'Keep an eye out for a motel. We'll take the first one we see.'

But the first was too big and brightly lit. The second, though, was perfect. Ten units huddled together on a narrow turn-off, behind a neon sign that blinked sadly into the moonless night. 'OTEL', it said, the missing letter like a gap in a tired old woman's smile.

'Our kind of place,' Peter said with a harsh laugh, as he pulled up to the office.

Sara put her hand on his arm just before he got out of the car. 'Be careful.'

He smiled at her for the first time in hours. 'Relax, love. We're still a good fifty miles from Brookville. And not even my parole officer would recognise me now.'

She watched as he stepped into the badly lit office. He'd exaggerated about the change in his appearance, she thought, but he did look different. His moustache was gone, of course, and she'd trimmed his hair short. Still, Sara didn't breathe easily until they were safely inside their motel room.

The room was like the sign outside—shabby and dim. Peter dropped their things on the lone chair and put his hands on his hips.

'Well,' he said finally, 'it's not the Laurentians, is it?'

'It's fine,' Sara said, trying not to notice the water-stained ceiling or the frayed carpet. The tinny sound of a television drifted through the thin wall separating their room from the next. 'It's just fine.'

Peter took a breath, and exhaled it slowly. 'Yeah. It's terrific.'

She watched as he circled the small room warily, drawing the curtains and double-locking the door, his body taut with apprehension, and then she ran her tongue across her lips.

'Peter? I was—I was thinking. Maybe we should go back.'

'Go back?'

She nodded. 'Yes. To Canada.' She moved towards him quickly. 'Maybe—maybe coming here wasn't such a good idea. Maybe——' Suddenly, the shrill wail of a police siren rent the air. The blood drained from her face. 'Oh, hell,' she whispered. 'The police. Peter, they've found us. They——'

He moved to her quickly, and took her into his arms. 'Easy,' he said, 'easy, sweetheart.'

She struggled against him. 'What's the matter with you? Don't you hear the siren? The police——'

'Sweet Sara,' he whispered, 'it's just the TV in the next room.' She stared at him, then pressed her face into his chest. His arms tightened around her, and he stroked her hair. 'It's all right, love. It's all right.'

When she had stopped shaking, she looked up at him and tried to smile.

'I'm sorry. I—I just keep thinking of what might happen.' An image of Peter locked behind iron bars danced through her mind, and she shuddered. 'I'm so afraid.'

A muscle moved in his jaw. 'Don't be,' he said fiercely. 'Don't ever be afraid, Sara. I won't let anything happen to you.'

She leaned back in his embrace and looked up at him. 'It's not that. It's——' But he wasn't listening. He was looking at her with an intensity that made her heart stop beating. 'What is it?' she whispered.

He answered by gathering her to him and kissing her, over and over, each kiss deeper and more passionate than the last. There was a desperation in his kisses that was almost frightening.

'Peter,' she murmured, 'what's wrong? Please, tell me.'

His hands cupped her face. 'Sara,' he whispered, 'my sweet Sara.'

He kissed her again, his mouth moving on hers with fierce hunger. There was something wrong, she could feel it, but, as he touched her, as he stripped her clothing away with rough urgency, she felt her body take fire from his. Her doubts fell away as desire swept through her.

'Yes,' she breathed, trembling against him. 'Yes,' she said again, and she reached to his shirt and began to undo the buttons, her fingers swift as they flew along the wool fabric.

Peter's mouth burned against her throat, against her breasts, and then he knelt before her and pulled her to him, his lips hot against her belly. Her head fell back, and she moaned as he kissed the tender inner flesh of her thighs.

He rose finally and took her hands in his. 'Undress me, Sara,' he whispered, bringing her hands to his belt.

She pulled away his clothing, pausing only to kiss his skin as she exposed it. He tasted of salt and desire; she savoured him with her tongue as if he were fine wine.

When he was naked against her, he swung her into his arms, and they fell on to the bed, locked together in a fierce embrace.

'Peter,' she whispered. 'Peter——'

'Shh,' he said, 'shh, sweet Sara.'

He kissed her as she arched against him, her body seeking the impalement that would make her his.

And, as she found it, a single, crystalline realisation pierced her heart.

I love you, Peter, she thought, and the seedy motel room became paradise.

Sara awoke to sunlight and muted sounds of traffic. 'Peter?' she murmured sleepily.

She was alone in the rumpled bed. She smiled and stretched lazily. Peter was in the shower; she could hear the sound of water running from behind the closed bathroom door.

Yesterday morning they had showered together, laughing beneath the warm spray, exploring with soap-slicked hands until the laughter became passion.

She smiled and pushed the blanket aside, imagining Peter's face when she drew back the curtain and stepped into the shower-stall with him. Afterwards, she would tell him what she'd started to tell him last night—that the scheme she had drawn him into was too dangerous.

Proving his innocence wasn't as important as keeping his freedom.

She padded silently to the bathroom door, and cracked it open an inch. The idea was to surprise him, but if she let the cold air in, he would know she was . . .

Her smile faltered. He wasn't in the shower; he was standing with his back to her. And he had the telephone in his hands. She looked down now, and saw the cord slithering beneath the door like a black snake.

'Yes,' he was saying, 'that's right, Eddie. I'll be in Chicago late tomorrow. I'll need papers.'

Of course! She should have known Peter would be one step ahead of her. Apparently, he'd decided their plan was too risky, just as she had. And he was already making alternate plans.

Chicago, she thought. She had never been to Chicago. And then where? Europe? South America? Not that it mattered. Just as long as she and Peter were together.

'Right, Eddie. A passport. A driver's licence. Hell, no. Just for me. Yeah, yeah, I know what the papers say. But I'll be travelling alone. It's—it's safer that way.'

She felt the clutch of a cold fist around her heart, and she stumbled back against the bedroom wall.

'I'll be travelling alone,' he'd said. No! Oh no, he was leaving her. How could he do that? How?

'It's safer that way,' he'd murmured.

Sara pressed her hand to her mouth. Was he right? She knew very little about evading the law, but . . .

She knew nothing about it. She was a handicap, a liability a man on the run could ill afford. Peter had to stop and explain everything to her; hadn't she gone to pieces last night, and all because of a siren on a stupid TV programme?

The water stopped abruptly.

'Sara?'

She stiffened. Peter was standing in the doorway to the bathroom, she could feel his eyes boring into her back. Quickly, she pulled on her clothes, her fingers trembling on the buttons and zips, and then she turned towards him. He looked at her narrowly.

'I didn't realise you were awake,' he said.

She nodded. 'I just got up. I heard the shower . . .'

They both looked at the telephone in his hands. Peter set it down carefully.

'I was on the phone,' he said. 'I thought you might have overheard me.'

Don't cry, she told herself fiercely. 'No,' she said, 'no, I didn't. I—I just got up.'

'Good. I mean, I'm glad I didn't disturb you. I—er—I had to call a hardware store.'

Sara stared at him. 'A hardware store?'

'Yeah.' He gave her a quick smile. 'I wanted to—to check on the things we'll need for Winstead's tonight.'

He wasn't going to tell her he was leaving. He was going to walk out of her life the same way he had walked into it.

'I—I found what I'll need,' he said. 'I have to go and get it.'

She swallowed past the lump in her throat. 'At the hardware store,' she said, and he nodded. 'I see.' Her voice trembled, and she pulled free of his hands and turned away. 'When?'

His hand brushed against her hair. 'Now.'

Now.

'Sara.' His voice grew husky. 'I—I wish . . .' She heard the ragged intake of his breath. 'There are things I haven't told you, things I'm not sure you would understand . . .'

But you have told me, she cried inside. 'The reward isn't worth the risk', you said. You can't face prison again, you said. And I understand, my love, I do.

He shook his head, as if he were impatient with himself. 'None of that matters now. I just wish—I wish there were some other way.' His hand brushed her hair again, lingering against her cheek. 'It's safer if I leave you here, Sara.'

She closed her eyes. Remember this, she thought,

remember the feel of his hand, the sound of his voice, the warmth of his breath. Remember this, because it's all you'll have for the rest of your life.

Tears welled behind her eyelids. I can't watch you walk out of that door, Peter, she screamed inside. I can't do it. I'll die if I have to see you go.

Quickly, before she could change her mind, Sara stepped away from him and snatched up her jacket.

'Sara? What are you doing?'

She pulled a pair of dark glasses from her pocket, and jammed them on her nose.

'I—I noticed some vending machines near the office when we drove in last night. I thought they might sell coffee.'

'Sara.' His voice was rough. 'Sara—wait a minute. Please.'

'You go on, Peter. I'll just get the coffee and wait for you here and—and . . .' Her voice broke and she wrenched the door open. 'Goodbye,' she whispered. *Goodbye, my love*.

'Sara, wait——'

She stepped out into the cold morning with the sound of his voice ringing after her. Tears blinded her as she trotted across the car park. Was Peter watching? She assumed he was, and she continued in a determined line towards a shadowed archway that housed a cluster of public telephone booths and food vending machines. This would have to be her hiding place, the place where she could give in to her pain.

She ducked into the archway and sagged against the nearest booth. Head bowed, she waited to hear the sound of the car door opening and slamming shut, the snarling whine of the starter bringing the Rover's engine to life. She waited for the crunch of gravel that would tell her Peter Saxon was pulling out of the car park and out of her life.

'Sara? Sara, thank heaven! Are you OK?'

A man's arm caught her and closed around her. Sara cried out as she looked into the familiar face of Chief of Police Jim Garrett.

Peter, she thought, and her eyes widened in horror. 'No!' she yelled, twisting against Garrett. 'No, no——'

His arm tightened around her. 'It's all right, Sara. Take it easy. You're safe now.'

Wildly, Sara looked around her. The car park was alive with police and state troopers. Guns and rifles bristled everywhere.

'Oh, hell!' Her voice broke. 'Jim, listen to me, you don't understand——'

'We had a damned lucky break. I gambled on Saxon shaving off his moustache, so I had posters made up of him without it. The night clerk spotted one on his way home this morning and called my office.'

'Jim, you have to listen. Peter isn't——'

'How the hell did you get away? We were worried about what would happen to you when we made our move.'

Sara's voice rose in panic. 'Dammit, you have to——'

'Here we go. The troopers are bringing the son of a bitch out now.' Garrett's arm tightened around her as she began to tremble. 'Don't be afraid, Sara. He's never going to hurt anybody again.'

The door to the room she and Peter had shared opened. Two troopers stepped outside with Peter between them: Peter chained and shackled like a wild beast, Peter with a thin streak of blood smeared beside his mouth.

Sara reached out as he walked towards where she stood, in the curve of Jim Garrett's arm.

'Peter,' she whispered.

His eyes met hers, and she knew that she would remember the ice in their depths for the rest of her life.

CHAPTER ELEVEN

THE SNOWSTORM that had blanketed the north-eastern United States had ended almost two weeks before, but remnants of it still remained. Huge drifts of snow, sculpted by the wind into a white-waved sea and preserved by sub-freezing temperatures, lined the narrow roads that led into Brookville. The streets of the town still bore traces of the storm, in the icy ramparts that separated the pavement from the street.

The weather had remained cold and overcast for the past week. The sun that had appeared on the morning of Peter's arrest had sunk behind a heavy cloud-bank, while Sara and Jim Garrett rode back to town. The sky had turned dark and threatening, and that was how each day had been ever since.

Seated at her desk in the police station, Sara sighed, and stared out of the window. There was a bread-truck parked across the way, outside the ShopQuick Market, just as it was every morning. She could see the postman walking his route, hurrying his steps a little so he could finish before the predicted snow began to fall.

Nothing had changed in Brookville. It was a realisation that had come to her again and again throughout the past days. The town looked exactly as it had all the years of Sara's life—which was, of course, as it should be.

It was only she who had changed, she who would never be the same again.

She had fallen in love with Peter Saxon and lost him, all in four short days. In the week since his capture she had thought of little else except Peter, and how he must hate her. The look in his eyes as they had led him away tormented her by day and haunted her at night, plucking her from dreams in which Peter held her in his arms and kissed her, to hurl her into the cruel reality of her cold and lonely bed.

She hadn't seen Peter since the morning of his arrest. Jim Garrett had driven her back to town, then led her from his car and into the police station. Reporters and photographers had been clustered outside; what had seemed like hundreds of questions had been shouted at her. Sara had turned away from everyone, burying her face in the police chief's protective shoulder, and never looking up until the door to his private office had swung shut after them.

Then, with surprising gentleness for a man his size, Garrett had eased her into the swivel-chair behind his desk and squatted beside her.

'Sara? Are you all right?'

It had taken all the strength she had to nod her head. 'Yes,' she had whispered.

'Are you sure? I can send for the doc if you think——'

'Chief,' Sara's eyes had met those of her boss, 'Peter didn't hurt me. I keep telling you that.'

Garrett had risen to his feet. 'He sure as hell did something,' he had said, his voice flat. 'All I've heard for the past hour is how I've arrested the wrong man.'

'That's right. Peter is innocent. He's not a thief. He——'

'Sara, for heaven's sake, take it easy, will you?'

Sara drew a deep breath. 'I want to see him. I *have* to see him. He thinks I turned him in, Chief. He thinks I——'

Garrett squatted beside her again, and took her hands

in his. 'It doesn't matter what he thinks, Sara. He can't hurt you any more. You don't have to worry.'

Sara snatched her hands away. 'Damn,' she said, anger roughening her voice, 'I *want* to see him.' Suddenly, tears filled her eyes and began to spill down her cheeks. 'Please,' she whispered, 'take me to him.'

Her boss looked at her as if he had never seen her before. 'You've been under a lot of strain,' he said finally. 'I'm going to call Alice. I'll need a statement from you, but it can wait until you've calmed down and gotten some rest.'

'I'll give you a statement right now. Peter's been framed. He didn't take the jewels. He——'

The look on Garrett's face was made up of equal parts of compassion and distaste, but his voice gave nothing away.

'Just take it easy until Alice gets here, OK? What you need is to talk to another woman. Maybe then we can make some sense out of all this.'

Sara nodded numbly. She watched as Garrett telephoned his wife. It was impossible to hear what he said—he turned his back to her and cupped his hand around the phone—but when Alice arrived she had a sympathetic look in her eyes, and a determined set to her mouth.

'Sara and I aren't going to talk in your office, Jim,' she said, and she slipped a comforting arm around Sara's waist. 'You come with me, dear. My car's out back. We'll go have ourselves a nice cup of tea and chat a little.'

As soon as they were outside, Sara turned to the older woman. 'Alice, please, take me to Peter.'

Chief Garrett's wife spoke to her as if she were soothing a child awakening from a bad dream.

'They're probably still doing all the paperwork. You

know how long these things take.' She smiled and opened the car door. 'There's plenty of time. We'll go to your house, and you can take a shower and change while I put the kettle on.' She glanced at Sara meaningfully. 'And then we'll talk.'

The two women had talked until Sara was hoarse, Alice listening so sympathetically that at first Sara thought she believed her.

'Do you understand now?' Sara finally asked. 'Peter Saxon is innocent. You have to make the chief listen to me, Alice. Maybe—maybe you could talk to him while I go to Peter.'

Alice patted Sara's hand. 'Drink your tea, dear. It's good for you.'

'Didn't you hear me? I have to see Peter. He thinks I turned him in. I can't go on letting him believe that.'

Alice's face twisted, shattering the illusion of compassion. 'That rat! What kind of man would put a woman through such an ordeal? And all to save his own neck! No wonder you're confused.'

Sara stared at the older woman in disbelief. 'Haven't you heard anything I said? I love Peter.' Her voice cracked with anguish. 'How could he have thought I would call the police?'

'Let him think it. It's the only way you can salvage your pride.' Alice sighed. 'Don't you see? He played on your sympathies for his own protection. It's like the time they arrested him—that woman he stole from wouldn't say anything against him either.'

Sara shook her head. 'The papers said she didn't see anything.'

'Maybe she just didn't *want* to see anything, the same as you.' Alice marched to the sink and filled the kettle with fresh water. 'Saxon was running out on you when Jim caught him. Do you really think he'd have done that if he cared anything for you?'

Sara bit her lip. 'He—he couldn't face prison. Put yourself in his place.'

'It's you I'm interested in,' Alice said, slamming the kettle down on the electric stove. 'A man like that ought to be horsewhipped. I hope they lock him up and throw away the key—and so will you, once you get some rest and come to your senses.'

Alice Garrett had been on the phone to her husband, her back to the kitchen, when Sara rose quietly and slipped out of the door. Her car had been sitting in the cold all week, but it started up easily. She had glanced in the mirror just in time to see the chief's wife running down the road after her, yelling at her to come back.

Sara had driven straight to the county gaol, only to be told that Peter Saxon refused to see her. He had refused her calls, too, the next day and the day after that.

The whole thing was like a nightmare. And there seemed nothing she could do to change it. Nothing . . .

'Sara?'

She blinked her eyes and looked up. The postman was standing before her desk, the morning's mail clutched in his hand.

'Sorry, Mr Pemberton. I didn't hear you come in.'

The man nodded. 'Snow in the air,' he said laconically.

'That's what the weather report says.'

The postman looked at her through eyes red-rimmed by the wind. 'Heard a rumour you refused to testify against that Saxon fella, Sara. Is that true?'

'Heard a rumour you're not gonna finish your route by nightfall, Eddie.' Sara looked behind her. Jim Garrett stood in the doorway to his private office, his grizzled eyebrows raised politely. 'Is that true?'

The postman shrugged, and put the mail into Sara's

outstretched hand. 'Town runs on rumours, Chief.' His eyes slid to Sara. 'We all know that.' He smiled and pulled up his collar. 'Have a good day, folks.'

'Same to you, Eddie.' Garrett stood behind Sara until the outer door had opened and closed. Then he sighed, and came around to the front of her desk. 'Maybe you shouldn't have come back to work just yet,' he said.

Sara shook her head. 'No,' she said quickly, 'no, I'd much rather be here than at home. The days were endless . . .'

. . . but not as endless as the nights, she thought.

Jim Garrett nodded. 'Yes, I guess you're right. Besides, in a town like this, there's not much you can do to stem gossip.' He gave Sara a sharp look. 'You do know people are beginning to talk, don't you?'

She smiled faintly. 'People always talk in Brookville, Chief. It's how they get through the winter.'

'I'm not joking, Sara. There are all kinds of rumours floating around. And it's only going to get worse. I can't put people off forever. They're full of questions.'

Sara shrugged her shoulders. 'I appreciate your concern, Chief, but I haven't asked you to protect me. Besides, everyone will know how I feel when the case comes to trial.'

Garrett perched his bulky haunches on the edge of her desk. 'I'm hoping you'll come to your senses long before then. The prosecutor is going to subpoena you. You'll have to go into a courtroom and testify under oath.'

'Peter Saxon didn't steal those jewels.'

'The judge won't solicit your opinion,' Garrett said sharply. 'He'll be interested in facts.'

'I'll tell what I know. Peter is innocent.'

Her boss sighed. 'Sara, listen to me. I don't know what happened between you and Saxon——'

Sara flushed. 'I told you what happened. We figured out the truth about the jewel theft.'

Garrett waved his hand in the air. 'I know, I know. Saxon was framed by Simon Winstead. You've been telling me that all week.' His eyes met hers. 'But the prosecutor's not going to buy that without proof, Sara. He's going to rake you over the coals if you try that story on him.'

Sara tossed down her pencil. 'What would you like me to do? Lie? Say that—that Peter stole the jewels? That he beat me? That he—that he——'

'I only want you to tell what you know. Saxon kidnapped you. He threatened you. He restrained you forcibly. He stole a car——'

Sara shoved back her chair and got to her feet. 'He had no choice. He was forced into doing those things, because he knew no one would believe him.'

Garrett's eyes narrowed. 'What the hell does that prove?'

'What it proves,' she said furiously, spinning towards him, 'is that he was right. I kept telling him to turn himself in. I said he would get a fair hearing from you, that you would put aside your prejudices and really listen to him.'

The chief scowled. 'Listen to him? I wish to hell I *could* listen to him. But he won't talk to me. The way I hear it, he's even refused to talk to his attorney. The only thing I know about this case is the crazy story I keep hearing from you—that Winstead set Saxon up, and that the missing jewels are in his safe.'

'It's not crazy,' Sara insisted. 'And I don't know why Peter hasn't said anything. He knows Winstead did it—it just doesn't make any sense.'

Jim Garrett sighed. 'None of this makes sense.'

Sara sank down at her desk. 'And it won't,' she said

wearily, 'not unless you look in Winstead's safe.'

'Back to square one,' the chief said. He watched her for a moment and then he cleared his throat. 'Alice and I were talking last night. We wondered, well, Alice thought—the thing is, we know you must have had a pretty bad time of it with Saxon. And people get turned around when they're under a lot of stress——'

Sara looked at him coldly. 'And?'

Garrett shrugged his shoulders. 'Maybe you should see somebody. I was talking to Doc Ronald, over at the hospital, and he says he knows somebody on staff there——'

Sara's eyebrows rose. 'Somebody? Don't you mean a psychiatrist?'

'What if he is? He's an expert on this kind of thing, the doc says. He can help you. He——'

'Dammit, I'm not crazy! I don't need a doctor—I need somebody to believe me.' Suddenly her anger dissolved, and was replaced by a bone-draining weariness. 'Chief, I beg you, get a search-warrant for the Winstead house. Open the safe.'

The police chief rolled his eyes to the ceiling. 'I wish to hell I could! I'm beginning to think that's the only way to make you see the truth.'

'Then why don't you?'

Garrett snorted. 'There's not a judge in the state who would grant me a warrant, Sara. You've been in this business long enough to know that.'

'But if you tell him . . .'

'Tell him what? That my secretary says Peter Saxon told her New York's classiest jeweller's got three million bucks' worth of stolen jewels stashed in his safe?' The big man made a face. 'Hell, Sara, just listen to yourself. I don't know how that S.O.B. got you to believe a story like that, but it's so full of holes, it couldn't hold a thimble full of water.'

Sara drew in her breath. 'I saw the jewels,' she said softly. 'I told you that.'

Garrett's eyes narrowed. 'In a tool-box, in the trunk of Saxon's car.'

'Yes. And——'

'And you noticed right away that the tiara and the emeralds were missing.'

Sara hesitated. 'No. Well, not exactly. Peter was the one who noticed. And he told me. And——'

The chief threw up his hands. 'For heaven's sake, can you just hear me telling that to a judge? "My secretary says Saxon told her some of the pieces were missing, Your Honour. And he told her he knows where they are."' He shook his head. 'Sara, for pity's sake——'

'Suppose—suppose I said I *had* noticed it right away? I mean, what if I'd realised that some of the jewels weren't there the first time I saw them?'

Garrett lowered his head. 'Do you know what you're saying?'

Her chin rose in defiance. 'Would it make a difference? Would you be able to get a warrant if——'

'No.' Her boss's voice was sharp. 'It wouldn't be worth a damn. For one thing, Saxon could have had the missing jewels in his pocket.'

Sara stared at him. 'But he didn't. He——'

'For another,' Garrett said coldly, 'I would know you were lying, because that's not the way you told me the story every other time we talked.' He stared at Sara until her cheeks coloured. 'So,' he said finally, 'you would even lie for that creep, would you?'

'Peter is innocent.'

The chief shook his head. 'I just can't believe it, Sara. You, of all people. Why? I always thought you could spot a phoney——' He shook his head. 'Look, why don't you come to stay with Alice and me for a while? Alice thinks——'

Sara turned away. 'I know what she thinks. She thinks that Peter Saxon made a fool of me.'

'No, Sara. Nothing like that.'

She drew a deep breath. 'I don't want him to be locked up for a crime he didn't commit. Anything else is my business, and no one else's.'

Garrett ran his fingers through his hair. 'Sara, the man doesn't deserve this kind of loyalty. He won't even see you.'

She laughed bitterly. 'I'm not the most popular woman in town, am I? Winstead won't see me, either.'

The chief's head rose sharply. 'What?'

'Don't lecture me, please. I know I shouldn't have done it.'

'Done what? Sara, for heaven's sake, if you've made insane accusations about Simon Winstead, he'll have your job and mine so fast that it'll make your head spin.'

She sighed and rose from her chair. 'Don't worry,' she said, pouring herself a cup of coffee. 'I didn't accuse him of anything. I drove to his house last night. His butler announced me, and Winstead came to the door just long enough to tell me not to show my face there again.'

Garrett put his hand to his forehead. 'Sara, hell, that wasn't bright at all. The man's got lawyers and——'

The shrill ring of the telephone cut him off. Sara reached for it, but he waved her away. She sipped her coffee as he lifted the receiver and mumbled his name into it. He listened for a moment, his face darkening, and then he slammed the phone down on the desk.

Sara put her cup down. 'Bad news?'

The big man shrugged. 'Just a minor set-back. That

was the state cops. They took Indian Lake Lodge apart, looking for the jewels.' His eyes met hers. 'They didn't find them.'

Sara nodded. 'I told you they wouldn't. I told that to Winstead last night, too. Not that he wanted to hear it.'

Garrett sighed. 'I thought he didn't talk to you.'

'He didn't. Not really. I told him Peter Saxon was no thief. And Winstead laughed and said he *was*, that honest people didn't drive around with tool-boxes full of jewels in the boots of their cars.'

Jim Garrett got to his feet. 'What? What did you just say, Sara?'

Sara looked at him, her expression puzzled. 'I said I told Winstead that Peter wasn't a thief.'

He shook his head impatiently. 'Not that. The other part.'

'The other . . .? Winstead said only a thief would have a tool-box full of jewels tucked in the boot of his car.' She stared at her boss's face, and her pulse suddenly began to race. 'Why are you looking at me that way?'

Garrett's meaty hands clasped her shoulders. 'Are you sure that's what he said? I mean, about the jewels being in the tool-box?' Sara nodded. 'That's very interesting,' he said softly. '*Very* interesting. You see, nobody but you and Saxon knew the jewels were in a tool-box.'

Her heart turned over. 'Are you sure?'

Jim Garrett nodded. 'Saxon hasn't made any statement at all. And you haven't spoken to anybody but me.'

'Jim.' Sara's voice was a whisper. 'The only way Simon Winstead could have known that . . .'

'. . . is if he put the jewels there himself.' The chief of police nodded his head slowly. 'All right,' he said after a minute, 'let's hear your crazy story again, Sara. From the top.' He looked out of the window to the snow that had begun falling, and a quick smile flashed across his face. 'What the hell? It's going to be a long afternoon. What have I got to lose?'

CHAPTER TWELVE

IT WAS amazing, Sara thought, how easily euphoria could change to despair.

Only a few hours ago, she'd been filled with hope. She'd told Jim Garrett the details of her flight with Peter over and over during the past six days, but this afternoon had been the first time she had done so with an eagerness that even she could hear in her voice. The chief listened closely, interrupting only after she'd described the moment she'd first seen the jewels in the boot of Peter's car, heaped in the tool-box, and gleaming like dime-store spangles under the beam of her flashlight.

'You're sure, Sara?'

Her eyes had met Garrett's. 'Yes.' She'd waited for her boss to say something more, but he hadn't, and finally she had cleared her throat. 'Are you convinced now? Winstead put the jewels there himself. He would never have known about the tool-box otherwise.'

The chief had shrugged. 'Maybe.'

That was when her euphoria had begun to fade. 'Maybe? But you said he did. You said——'

'I said it was an interesting possibility.'

'He put them there, Chief. You know he did.'

Her boss had given her a non-committal smile. 'Maybe, Sara. That's the best I'm going to do right now. I'll check it out, and if I can come up with something——'

'What do you mean, you'll check it out? I just gave you all the proof you need. I——'

Garrett had shoved back his chair, risen heavily to his feet, and strolled to the window.

'The snow's picking up. Why don't you go on home before the roads get any worse?' When he had turned towards her and seen the look on her face, he had sighed. 'If I come up with something, I'll let you know. *If*, Sara. Do you understand?'

Sara had nodded without enthusiasm. 'Sure. I understand.'

Now, hours later, she was sure she did. Simon Winstead was a clever man. He had probably come up with some reasonable explanation for what he'd said about the jewels being in the tool-box. Actually, now that she thought about it, all he had to do was deny ever having made the remark.

It was only her word against his. And considering the way she had behaved over the past few days, her credibility was hardly better than Peter's.

Sara sighed deeply, drained the last drops of tea from her cup, and set it down on the table beside the couch. There had to be a way to prove Peter's innocence, just as there had to be a way to convince him that she hadn't betrayed him. At first, she'd wondered which pained her more—remembering the way he had looked at her as the troopers took him away, or knowing he was in gaol.

But, as the days went by, she knew which was the worst. It was that Peter was behind bars, caged like an animal.

'I thought I'd die in there.'

She could still hear him telling her that, still see the darkness in his eyes.

She rose quickly, and pulled her fleecy robe more closely around her body. She would confront Winstead again tomorrow, and find a way to get him to make the damning admission again. Only this time she would be ready. She would bury a tape recorder in her bag. Or she would beg Chief Garrett to go with her. Or she would . . . she would . . .

Sara let out her breath. There had to be a way. She was just too tired to think of it now. It seemed days and days since she'd slept.

She sighed and looked at the grey cat curled on the couch. 'Come on, Taj,' she murmured. 'It's bedtime.' The animal looked up, yawned delicately, then put its head down again and closed its eyes. Sara smiled. 'I don't blame you. I guess I've been keeping you awake at nights, haven't I?'

She stroked the silken little body, then switched out the light. The house was plunged into darkness, and she felt a sudden unpleasant chill, as if there were a draught blowing in through an open window. No, she thought suddenly, it wasn't that. It was as if . . . as if someone were out there in the dark, watching and waiting.

She made a quick circuit of the rooms, checking that all the windows and doors were securely bolted. They were—and yet the uncomfortable feeling remained.

'You need a good night's sleep, Sara Mitchell,' she said with determination, and then she scooped up the cat and started up the stairs. The cat protested softly, miaowing its displeasure at being disturbed. 'Sorry, pussycat,' Sara said, stroking the soft grey fur. 'I just don't feel like being alone.'

She shivered when she reached her bedroom. It was cold in here, too, which was strange because she had the heat turned up. But there was a lack of warmth in the house tonight. Everything seemed foreign, and somewhat out of kilter.

She shook her head impatiently. That was all she needed now—an over-active imagination to add to everything else. She put the cat on the bed. It miaowed, leaped off, and disappeared into the dark hall.

'OK,' Sara called after it, 'go on, be a cat. Assert your independence. See if I care.'

She paused beside the window, and stared out into the night. The snowfall was thick and heavy, lying over the gently sloping hills and skeletal trees like a white blanket. Above, the moon cast a cold light across the sky.

Peter had carried her off on a night like this. There had been no moon then, but the snow had fallen all around them, enclosing them in a soft cocoon. Would she ever be able to look at snow again without this terrible pain in her heart?

She bowed her head and pressed it against the window. The glass was cold; ice flowers bloomed on it, the chill fruit of the winter night.

'I love you, Peter.'

Her whispered words trembled in the silence. If only she hadn't talked him into coming back to the States. If only he would see her, and let her explain what had happened . . .

Impatiently, she pulled the heavy curtains closed, and turned away from the window. What did it matter now? You couldn't go back and undo what was; you could only work to change the future. And that, Sara thought, as she slipped off her robe and climbed into bed, was what she would do.

She switched off the bedside-light and lay back on the pillow. Somehow, she would find a way to free Peter. She would tell him she loved him. She would tell him she had not betrayed him. She . . .

Slowly, her lashes fell to her cheeks. The wind moaned softly through the skeletal trees.

Sara slept.

* * *

. . . No man had ever touched her like this before. No man had ever kissed her in this way, or whispered these things to her. She was blooming like a desert flower under the sweetness of a sudden rainshower, alive and eager for what Peter offered. Her mouth was filled with the taste of him, her breasts swelled beneath his caress, her body arched against his.

Peter's calloused fingers brushed the smooth column of her throat, and his hand slipped into her hair, his fingers tangling in the blonde strands as he drew her head back. He bent to her again, and she moaned as she felt the silken slide of his tongue against hers. Her senses blazed with the heat of his love . . .

She was dreaming. She knew she was dreaming, the message filtering through some separate, clear-thinking part of her mind. But the dream was so wonderful. If only it could last forever. If only . . .

'Sara.'

She sighed in her sleep. Peter's voice was soft; she could even feel the warmth of his breath against her cheek.

I love you, Peter . . .

'Sara.' Hands clasped her shoulders and lifted her. 'Sara. Wake up.' She felt the brush of fingers against her skin.

Her eyes flew open. 'Peter?' Her voice was soft with sleep, disbelieving. 'Peter,' she said again, and her heart filled with a rush of joy.

This was no dream. He was here. Peter was here, in her room, sitting on the bed beside her. He had opened the curtains; in the pale glow of moonlight, she could just make out his shadowed features, the strong line of cheek and jaw.

He drew back as she reached out to him. 'Hello, Sara.'

'I can't believe it,' she whispered. 'How did you—what are you doing here? You——' Her heart thudded wildly. 'You escaped from gaol. Oh, Peter——'

His face hardened. 'Did you really think you were safe from me, Sara? You should have known I would find a way to reach you.'

'You escaped,' she said again, and her eyes lit with alarm. Quickly, she pushed the blankets aside, and swung her legs to the floor. 'You've got to hurry,' she whispered. 'They're sure to come here.'

His hands closed tightly on her shoulders. 'Where the hell do you think you're going?'

Sara stared at him. 'There's no time to waste,' she said. 'They'll come here, Peter. And when they do——'

She winced as the pressure of his fingers increased. 'That's not going to save you,' he growled.

'Peter, please——'

'You sold me out, Sara.'

'No,' she said quickly, 'no, that's not true. I know you think I did, but——'

'Don't play games with me, dammit.' His voice was cruel with anger. 'You sold me out, and now you're going to pay for it. I've been waiting for this moment, Sara. It's what kept me from going insane inside that cage.'

Dark wings of fear fluttered in her breast. In the eerie, ice-blue wash of moonlight that filled the room, she could see his face clearly. There was a coldness in his eyes she had only seen once before, in the car park outside the motel, as the troopers had led him away.

'Peter, listen to me. It's not what you think——'

His lips drew away from his teeth. 'Listen to you?' he whispered. 'I *did* listen to you, and look where it got me.'

'If you would just let me explain——'

'I never had a chance to pay you back for your advice, Sara.' Again, he smiled that terrible smile. 'But I will tonight.'

The unspoken threat sent a chill along her flesh. There was a dark side to Peter—how had she forgotten? She remembered how he'd run after her and caught her in the bank car park the night he'd kidnapped her, how easily he had become part of Frenchy Nolan's world, in that sleazy bar in Montreal.

He had spent sixteen months in prison, experiencing things she had never even dreamed of.

He could be ruthless when he had to be.

He was a man on the run, and he thought she'd betrayed him. It was a combination that might lead to almost anything.

'How the hell could you have sold me out?' His hands tightened on her. 'I've gone through it a thousand times——'

Her fear took a new focus as she looked past him to the face of the bedside clock over his shoulder. It was just past two in the morning. How long had he been here? Ten minutes? Fifteen? Had they discovered his absence from the gaol by now?

How long did he have before the manhunt for him began? How long would it be before her house was surrounded by car-loads of troopers and men with dogs straining at the ends of their leads, their muzzles flecked with foam?

'Peter.' Her voice cut through his. 'Peter, please, there's no time for this. You have to get away. They'll look here. They'll come here first.'

'Don't count on it, Sara.'

She shook her head. 'They will. Garrett knows how I feel about . . . he knows what I'll do. He——'

She cried out as his hands clasped her more tightly. 'Yes,' he whispered, 'I'll bet he does.'

Something wailed thinly, far in the distance. Sara caught her breath and listened. Was it a police siren? No, she thought, closing her eyes with relief, no, it was a train, whistling mournfully into the night. There was still time.

'Listen to me, Peter. My car is in the garage. I'll bring it around and——'

He laughed. 'Terrific. The last time you trotted off to buy coffee. This time you're going off to get the car.' His fingers bit into her flesh. 'Don't waste your time, sweetheart. There aren't any telephone booths handy tonight—and I've cut the line to yours.'

Sara stared at him. 'Is that what you think? That I want to turn you in?'

'Again.' His lips drew back from his teeth. 'You left that out, sweet Sara. But it won't work this time.'

A slow flush of anger heated her blood. She was dizzy with schemes to save him, and all he could think of was her supposed duplicity.

'Listen,' she said softly, 'this isn't the time. But you're wrong about me. And I'm beginning to resent——'

'You're damned right I was wrong about you!' Peter's jaw shot forward. 'Damn, but you had me fooled. It was just kicks, wasn't it? Little Sara Mitchell got the chance to spread her wings for the first time in her life, and she liked the feeling. And then——'

'What are you talking about? I——'

Peter's eyes darkened, and his hands slid down her flannel-sleeved arms. 'You really got through to me, Sara. Isn't that a laugh?' His fingers curled around her wrists. 'For the very first time, I almost regretted what I'd done. I found myself wondering what it would be like if I could go back and undo——'

Sara stared at him. 'There was nothing to undo, Peter. You didn't steal the jewels of the Maharanee of Gadjapur—we both know that.'

A smile twisted across his face. 'You don't understand, Sara. I never stole *any* jewels. None, not ever, not at the Winstead party or anywhere else.'

What was he talking about? Peter was a thief. A reformed thief, yes, but . . .

His head bent towards hers. 'Johnny was the cat burglar.' His eyes darkened with pain. 'We'd played the game too long, you see; we kept playing it after that first night, and after a while it became too important to him. He couldn't stop——'

Sara was almost afraid to breathe. 'But if your brother was the thief—if it wasn't you——'

Peter's breath hissed between his teeth and she knew, from the look on his face, that he hadn't heard her.

'It was fun, at first.' He laughed softly. 'Hell, fun isn't the right word. It was exciting, it was—it was the biggest kick in the world. We got good at it—after a while, there wasn't an office on campus we hadn't been in. We moved our raids into the city——'

'The foreign embassies?'

His teeth flashed in a feral smile. 'No security system could stop us. We were invincible.' His hands fell away from her; Sara watched, spellbound, as he stared beyond her into the darkness. 'And each time, Johnny took something. Never much, not then. A notepad. A book of matches——'

Sara stared at him. 'But it changed,' she said, knowing instinctively what came next. 'Stationery and matches weren't enough.'

Peter nodded. 'Yes. And that's when I realised the game had gotten out of hand, that we had to stop. I told

Johnny. He laughed at first, but I said—I said that was how it had to be. It was over, I told him. I wanted out.' He drew a shuddering breath. 'But it wasn't over, not for him. I should have known. I should have suspected——'

Sara got to her feet and put her hand on his arm. 'Peter——'

'I went to his apartment the night he was killed. I had a key; I just wanted to be in a place that was filled with his spirit.' He shrugged free of her hand. 'It was all there, in his bedroom. The jewels he'd stolen, the newspaper clippings about the thefts and the daring cat burglar who had pulled them off.' Pain knifed across his face. 'I almost went crazy, trying to think of a way to protect him from what would happen when the papers got hold of the story. At first I thought I would toss it all in a sewer.'

'But you didn't,' Sara whispered. 'You decided to return the jewels.'

Peter laughed. 'Crazy, right?' The smile fled his face. 'Maybe I *was* crazy that night. All I know is, it went wrong right away. There was an emerald locket on a gold chain—I recognised it, it belonged to a woman Johnny and I had both dated. In fact, I'd seen her wearing it two nights before. She was away for the weekend, I knew that, too. And I thought, hell, she doesn't even know the locket's gone. If I can just return it before she gets back——'

'But you got caught.'

He laughed again. 'Yes. She'd come home early. I'd played the game a hundred times before, but the one time it really mattered, I got caught.'

Sara stared at him. 'And you let the police think it was you all along.'

He nodded. 'It was the last thing I could think of

doing for my brother,' he said softly. 'It was all that was left.'

The room filled with silence. After a few moments, Sara sighed deeply.

'You must have loved him a lot,' she murmured.

Peter swung towards her with a speed that made her flinch. 'Yes,' he growled, catching her by the shoulders, 'I loved him. He was all I had. And I never once looked back. I never regretted a minute of it, not the trial, or the contempt in my grandfather's face, or even the endless hell of prison . . .' His hands bit into her flesh. 'Until that night in that fleabag motel, Sara. That was the first time I found myself thinking maybe what I'd done had been a mistake, that if I'd never let the world think I was a thief, I wouldn't have ended up in a mess with no way out.'

'There *was* a way out,' said Sara. 'And you took it. I don't blame you for running off, Peter. You couldn't face prison.'

'Come on, Sara.' His mouth narrowed. 'I wasn't the one who ran off. *You* were. You heard me on the phone that morning, and you leaped to the conclusion that I was leaving you because I didn't need you any more. I know that's what happened; you might as well admit it.'

Sara drew in her breath. 'Yes, I heard you. But I never thought that, not for a minute. I heard what you said about it being safer to travel alone. And I understood, Peter.' Her eyes met his. 'I knew how determined you were not to get caught. I knew you regretted the scheme I'd talked you into. I——'

'You're damned right I was determined not to get caught! You would have been an accessory. If they found us breaking into Winstead's house, you would have gone to gaol. And I would have died before I let that happen to you.'

What was he saying? Sara stared at him in disbelief. 'You mean, you were afraid for me, not yourself?'

'I couldn't let you run a risk like that.' Peter's eyes darkened. 'I've been in a cage, remember? I know what it's like.'

She ran her tongue over her lips. 'Then why—why didn't you say something? Why didn't you ask the man on the phone to make up new papers for the two of us?'

Peter's hands slipped from her shoulders, up her throat to her face. His fingers threaded into her hair.

'That's what I was going to do. I thought about it while we were driving towards Brookville. But then we got to the motel; I looked at you in that dingy little room, I saw the terror on your beautiful face when you thought the cops were after us, and I knew I loved you too much to drag you into that kind of life with me.'

She looked into his eyes. It was all too incredible to be true. He loved her. He had been leaving her only *because* he loved her.

'Why didn't you tell me?' she whispered.

'What right did I have to tell you I loved you?' he demanded. 'What could I have offered you?'

'Your love is enough,' Sara said. 'It's all I want——'

Suddenly, his face twisted in pain. 'How could you have turned me in, Sara? Didn't what we'd shared mean anything to you?'

'It meant everything. I love you so much, Peter. I——'

'You heard me on the phone, you heard me making plans to leave and, right away, you thought the worst.' He shook his head. 'Hell, you thought the worst all along. Each time I tried to tell you how I felt about you, you accused me of trying to use you.'

'I think I was just afraid to believe you cared for me. It was all like a dream.'

He tilted her face to his. 'Why didn't you tell me you'd heard me make that call? Why didn't you ask me to explain?'

Sara shook her head. 'I didn't want to complicate things for you, Peter. I thought—I thought that's how you wanted it. Don't you understand? I love you.'

His eyes grew dark. 'Don't keep saying that,' he said in a fierce whisper. 'You're just trying to save yourself now. You don't love me. If you did, you would never have betrayed me.'

Sara put her fingers to his lips. 'I didn't betray you. I didn't call the police. It was the desk clerk—he recognised you.' She looked into his eyes. 'I would never do anything to hurt you.'

He drew in his breath, then let it out in a ragged sigh. 'I want so damned much to believe you, Sara.'

'You *have* to believe me,' she said urgently. 'We have to get out of here, Peter. They'll be coming after you, and Jim Garrett will know to look here.'

'Garrett? What do you mean?'

Quickly, she began undoing the tiny buttons that ran down the bodice of her flannel gown.

'I told him everything. That I love you. That Winstead's the real thief. That we came back to Brookville to break into his safe.' She tilted her head to the side. 'You didn't tell anyone that, though.'

'No.' Peter gave her a quick smile. 'I kept telling myself I hated you—but I didn't want to implicate you. And I knew no one would believe me if I said Winstead was guilty.'

She nodded. 'You were right. Jim Garrett thought I was crazy when I tried to tell him about Winstead—although for a while I thought I'd finally found some proof he would accept.' She opened the last button and looked at Peter. 'Winstead made a slip of the tongue the other day. He told me—well, it doesn't matter now. But I got the chief to agree to try and get the truth out of him.'

'And?'

'And it didn't work. Or maybe the chief didn't bother.' Her voice grew muffled as she pulled the nightgown over her head. 'It doesn't matter,' she said, tossing the gown aside. 'What we have to do now is hurry. The police——' She paused and looked at him. 'Maybe later it would help if you told Jim the truth about your brother,' she said softly. 'But you won't, will you?'

A muscle tightened in Peter's jaw. 'No. Johnny's dead, and I've paid his debt. That part of my life—and his—is over. In fact, I've finally decided what to do with the rest of the things he . . . he took. I have it all in a vault, along with the newspaper clippings. I'm going to mail everything back to its rightful owners.'

Sara's breath caught. 'Anonymously,' she said quickly.

Peter laughed. 'Very anonymously.'

She let out her breath. 'Good. We can work out the details later. There isn't time now. We——' She frowned as Peter chuckled softly. 'What is it? Peter?'

He was looking at her so strangely. Where was the coldness she had seen in his eyes? Even the furrowed lines the past days had etched beside his mouth had eased away. He smiled lazily.

'No modesty at all, Miss Mitchell,' he said softly. 'There you were, all nice and proper in that floor-to-neck granny-gown——'

Sara looked down at herself, and then at him. A blush spread over her cheeks, and she snatched up the discarded gown and held it in front of her as Peter walked slowly towards her.

'For goodness' sake,' she said, 'am I the only one of us who's thinking straight? Chief Garrett——'

'Chief Garrett is probably tucked into his bed, where all intelligent people should be on a night like this.' Peter reached out and caught hold of the nightgown. He tugged at it lightly. 'You could catch a chill like that, Sara. Whatever are you thinking of?'

She clutched at the gown and stared at him. 'Chief Garrett won't be in his bed once he gets word you've broken out of gaol. Why are you looking at me like that?'

Peter grinned. 'I left that gaol the same way I entered it, love. Through the front door—only this time, there were no handcuffs on my wrists.'

'You mean the judge finally agreed to grant you bail?'

He shook his head. 'Something much better.'

Sara touched her tongue to her lips. 'Peter, don't tease me. What are you talking about?'

His fingers curled into the flannel gown. 'I'm free, Sara.'

The simple words were the most beautiful she had ever heard. 'Free?' she repeated in an incredulous whisper.

Peter smiled. 'They dropped all charges. I didn't get the whole story; I was too busy thinking about what I was going to do to you when I found you. But it had something to do with Garrett getting a full confession from Simon Winstead, after the jeweller let slip something incriminating.' His smile softened, as he tugged the gown from her nerveless fingers and dropped it to the floor. 'Your handiwork, apparently, Miss Mitchell.'

Sara drew in her breath. 'Oh, Peter——'

'Winstead, it turns out, ran up some heavy-duty

gambling debts. He needed money—lots of money. So he decided to steal his own jewels, and use me as a fall-guy.' Peter's arms closed slowly around her. 'And it would have worked, except for you.'

'It's over, then.'

He nodded. 'It's over.'

She closed her eyes. 'I can hardly believe it. I——' Her eyes flew open, and she stared at him. 'Peter—what are you doing?'

His hands spread along her naked back. 'You're cold,' he said with artful innocence. 'I'm just trying to see what we can do to warm you up.'

A slow sweetness spread through her limbs. 'Just a minute,' she said. 'You have some explaining to do yourself, Peter Saxon. How could you have thought I'd called the police?'

He smiled. 'I'll find some way to apologise,' he said. He drew her closer and kissed her throat. 'There's got to be a way to make it up to you.'

Her eyes closed as his lips moved to her earlobe. 'And—and what you said before, about what you were going to do to me when you found me——'

His mouth closed over hers. 'Yes,' he whispered, when he finally raised his head, 'I spent a lot of time on that. The trouble was, my ideas all kept running in this general direction.'

Sara's heart was racing against his. 'That's all right,' she said breathlessly. 'It's a pretty nice direction.'

He laughed, as he swung her into his arms and walked to the bed. 'You really are shameless,' he said, sitting down with her in his lap. 'Just the kind of woman a man like me needs.'

Sara's eyes sought his. 'Am I?' Her teasing smile fled. 'I want to be, Peter. I want to be all you'll need to make you happy for the rest of your life.'

Laughter danced in his eyes. 'Is that a proposal?'

Reach out and take the chance, Sara.

She drew in her breath. 'Yes.'

Peter smiled, but his eyes were serious. 'You would marry an ex-con like me?'

Sara lay her hand against his cheek. 'You mean, would I marry a man who gave up everything for love and honour?' She smiled. 'Yes, my darling, I would.'

His smile became a grin. 'I accept.'

Her heart filled with happiness. 'Are you sure?'

He kissed her with a slow, sweet passion that left her breathless. 'Does that convince you, sweet Sara?'

Sara smiled up at him. 'Well,' she said in a teasing whisper, 'it's a start.'

Her last thought, as Peter drew her down beside him, was that no eagle had ever flown higher than she and the man in her arms.

TASTY FOOD COMPETITION!

How would you like a years supply of Mills & Boon Romances ABSOLUTELY FREE? Well, you can win them! All you have to do is complete the word puzzle below and send it in to us by March. 31st. 1990. The first 5 correct entries picked out of the bag after that date will win **a years supply of Mills & Boon Romances** (*ten books every month - worth £162*) What could be easier?

H	O	L	L	A	N	D	A	I	S	E	R
E	Y	E	G	G	O	W	H	A	O	H	A
R	S	E	E	C	L	A	I	R	U	C	T
B	T	K	K	A	E	T	S	I	F	I	A
E	E	T	I	S	M	A	L	C	F	U	T
U	R	C	M	T	L	H	E	E	L	Q	O
G	S	I	U	T	F	O	N	O	E	D	U
N	H	L	S	A	T	O	N	E	F	M	I
I	S	R	S	O	M	A	C	W	A	A	L
R	I	A	E	E	T	I	R	J	A	E	L
E	F	G	L	L	P	T	O	T	V	R	E
M	O	U	S	S	E	E	O	D	O	C	P

CLAM	HOLLANDAISE	OYSTERS	SPICE
COD	JAM	PRAWN	STEAK
CREAM	LEEK	QUICHE	TART
ECLAIR	LEMON	RATATOUILLE	
EGG	MELON	RICE	
FISH	MERINGUE	RISOTTO	**PLEASE TURN**
GARLIC	MOUSSE	SALT	**OVER FOR**
HERB	MUSSELS	SOUFFLE	**DETAILS**
			ON HOW
			TO ENTER

HOW TO ENTER

All the words listed overleaf, below the word puzzle, are hidden in the grid. You can find them by reading the letters forward, backwards, up or down, or diagonally. When you find a word, circle it or put a line through it, the remaining letters (which you can read from left to right, from the top of the puzzle through to the bottom) will ask a romantic question.

After you have filled in all the words, don't forget to fill in your name and address in the space provided and pop this page in an envelope (you don't need a stamp) and post it today. Hurry - competition ends March 31st 1990.

Mills & Boon Competition,
FREEPOST,
P.O. Box 236,
Croydon,
Surrey. CR9 9EL
Only one entry per household

Hidden Question _____

_____

Name _____

Address _____

_____

_____

_____ Postcode _____

You may be mailed with other offers as a result of this application.

COMP 8